CORPSE REVIVER

SPECTRAL DETECTIVE: BOOK TWO

DAVID BUSSELL

Copyright © 2017 by David Bussell and Uncanny Kingdom.

All rights reserved.

No part of this book may be reproduced in any form or by any electronic or mechanical means, including information storage and retrieval systems, without written permission from the author, except for the use of brief quotations in a book review.

This is a work of fiction. Names, characters, businesses, places, events, and incidents are either the products of the author's imagination or used in a fictitious manner. Any resemblance to actual events, or to actual persons living, dead, or undead, is purely coincidental.

CORPSE REVIVER

1

All around town, artists were dying.

Dying from electrocutions, from hit and runs, and unexplained heart attacks. Dying from falling objects, from bathtub drownings, and walking into open lift shafts. All of the deaths considered suspicious, but none of them suspicious enough to be ruled homicide. I might have side-stepped them myself if the deceased had been your rinky-dink, Camden Market artists selling affordable Banksy ripoffs and blown glass bongs, but these artists were the real deal. High profile painters, sculptors, and whatever the ones that shit the bed and call it an "installation" go by. Big-name artists, falling like dominoes, and I had an inkling I knew who was doing the pushing.

A good place to start with any crime is to question the motive, and sometimes, a lot of the time, most of the time, that motive is money. So I got to thinking, who was it that stood to profit the most from putting these artists to bed with a shovel?

The buyers.

The art lovers who measured their love in pennies and

pounds. The collectors who cared less about art appreciation than they did the appreciation of their assets. And what better way to see those assets mature than for the artist who created them to suffer a premature death? The kind that caught the marketplace by total surprise and drove the value of their work sky high. The man who owned a work like that—the work of a famous, tragically defunct artist—would stand to make a tidy sum. The man who owned the work of two? Three? A dozen even? He'd be a millionaire a few times over. And a fucking suspect millionaire at that.

That's how it is when a famous artist croaks; it's like their departure trips some kind of mystical inflation switch. A death bump, if you like. It stood to reason that a collector had a hand in these murders, the only question was, which one? Since no one else was asking, I decided to make the investigation my own and find out.

I had a sniff around. Looked into certain private records, questioned dealers and gallery owners, greased the right palms. And one name kept coming up (well, not a name exactly, a face; the buyer was smart enough to make his purchases using aliases). Picture a London-based artist who died an untimely death in the last ten years and this guy, whoever he was, owned a piece of their work. Their masterpiece in most cases. The guy was making money hand over fist, and something told me he was more than just a canny investor.

If all of this sounds like some tin foil hat, swivel-eyed-loon conspiracy theory, I promise it only gets worse from here. Why wouldn't it? After all, you're reading the words of someone who's witnessed actual demons and visited the nightmare realm of an inter-dimensional being that steals children's souls. Oh, and I'm a ghost too, as in a real-life, walking the Earth, honest to goodness, phantom. I guess what I'm saying is, don't expect the needle of your internal Bullshit-O-Meter to sit too still on my watch.

Anyway, back to my art assassin case. Seeing as I didn't have the killer's ID, I figured the best chance I had of rounding him up was to catch the guy in the act. Ordinarily, I'd lay some bait—cast out a line and see if any sharks came biting—but since I didn't have anything in my chum bucket tasty enough to attract one, I had to go a different way this time.

Instead of waiting for the killer to come to me, I went straight to the source. I found the hottest artist in town, glommed on to the guy, and became his invisible protector. Since the police didn't have the resources to play bodyguard for some gadabout artiste, I made it my job to keep an eye on him. It wasn't an easy gig, but being a ghost means I don't need sleep, so I was able to monitor him around the clock. Without the artist knowing about it, I'd been on him for the past eight weeks, glued to his tail while he swanned about town like he owned the place. A typical day in his company would involve me traipsing around after him as he went from brunch to lunch to elevenses, interspersed every few days with a flying visit to his studio to ensure that his assistants executed *"his"* work according to something he had the brass to call, "My vision".

Eight long weeks of that I'd suffered, hoping like mad that the artist's would-be killer made a show, and caring less about whether he succeeded in slaying my protectee each passing day. Just being in the guy's presence was torture. Not only was he an utter prat of a man, he picked his nose, sucked his thumb, and ate an apple so loud that I twice thought about offing him myself.

The artist's name was Cassey Levant, a sculptor fascinated by the endless oscillation of the zeitgeist, at least according to the artsy bollocks some poor sod had been tasked with transferring letter by letter on to the gallery wall. Tonight was the grand opening of his ten-year retrospective, a glittering, champagne reception attended by some of the biggest dickheads in town. Truly, a Who's Who of the least essential members of contemporary London society.

As Levant strutted about like a peacock I watched the crowd, looking for any signs of impending danger and guarding his six like some supernatural secret service agent. I certainly looked the part in my black suit and tie; the outfit I happened to be wearing the day I died and consequently my permanent fashion choice.

My phone buzzed. I answered the call and a voice only I could hear came through the speaker.

'Anything to report?' asked Stella.

Stella was working as my partner this evening, watching the outside of the venue while I kept an eye on the inside. My phone had been enchanted by my magician friend, Jazz Hands, who functioned as my sort of paranormal 'Q,' equipping me with items fit for my phantom hands. I have trouble interacting with regular physical objects – my natural state is ethereal, so manipulating the real world is like trying to win a prize on one of those fairground claw machines. A shop-bought phone in these paws would have more cracks in it than a plumber's convention.

I scanned the room. 'Nothing yet,' I sighed.

No one besides Stella heard me talking. My voice and movements are inaudible to anyone not tuned into the Uncanny, by which I mean normals. And by "normals" I mean the regular people, the hoi-polloi, the bus-takers. Basically, you.

'Stay on it,' said Stella. 'Keep the line open and maintain contact.'

She sounded like someone from a bloody Andy McNab novel. I thought about ribbing her for it but gave her a simple, 'Affirmative,' instead. Stella's good at what she does, the best really, but she's not much for levity.

The night crept on. Levant quaffed champagne and pressed the flesh as his adoring fans heaped praise upon his latest sculptures, which looked less like art than an explosion in a mannequin factory to me.

I was beginning to think the evening was a bust when a burly man in an unseasonably large overcoat happened on to the scene. As he made a beeline for Levant I saw his hand go for the inside pocket of his coat, and readied myself to turn corporeal and knock whatever weapon he was packing from his grip.

Levant's eyes went wide as he saw the man barreling up to him.

I darted forwards, desperate to stop the killer before he could make his move and then—

'Daaahling!' squealed Levant.

The man in the coat met him in a big queeny hug and a flurry of air kisses before telling Levant how absolutely *stunning* he looked this evening.

Great. Instead of bringing down a serial killer I'd been a half-second away from clotheslining some hapless art ponce.

The burly man handed his coat to a lackey, who gave him a ticket and squirrelled it away in the cloakroom. The man went on to tell Levant that this was his finest work yet, and how every piece on display was a great, crashing triumph.

'My God!' he gushed, looking around. 'Did you manage to hawk the entire collection?'

'Not quite,' replied Levant, gesturing to a mannequin with a head sculpted to look like a poop emoji for reasons I could not possibly fathom. 'This piece remains stubbornly unsold.'

'What do you mean?' asked the sycophant. 'It has a red dot right there...'

I followed his chubby index finger to the piece's caption card, which had indeed been decorated with a little red dot.

Except—

The red dot was moving—

Vacating its position on the white rectangle to travel along the gallery wall—

Creeping in the direction of Cassey Levant.

It wasn't a red dot.

Well, it was, but not the kind you peeled from a pack of stickers.

It was the kind that killed.

I turned from the dot and saw a slim, red beam passing through the gallery's south window.

Outside, across the road, and projecting from the mid-level of a multi-storey car park, was the source of the beam – a laser sight fixed to the barrel of a sniper rifle. Holding on to that rifle was a dead match for my suspect.

I turned back to see the laser's red dot had finished its journey and arrived on the gunman's target. Levant just stood there like a plum, mouth agape as the scarlet bead settled on the dead centre of his forehead. If somebody didn't do something fast, the gunman's stock was about to rise as quickly as Levant's body fell.

'Everybody down!' I yelled, though of course, no one heard me.

To make up for the intellectual shortfall, I dived into the fray like a goalkeeper. Having succeeded in turning my shoulder corporeal, I collided with Levant's back and sent him buckling to the gallery's faux-marble floor.

There was a popping noise, quickly followed by the sound of shattering glass and the appearance of a smoking bullet hole in the mannequin's poop head.

Then came bedlam.

Champagne flutes rained to the ground as screaming art lovers ran for cover, swarming to the room's only exit and arriving at a crush in the stairwell. Stunned, Levant rolled on to his knees and went looking for his guardian angel, but found the room empty except for himself. The luvvie he'd been air-kissing moments ago was long gone, rushing to get clear of the building with all the rest. Only me and my perspiring artist left now – and Stella, watching from her post outside.

I scanned the multi-storey across the road and whipped out my phone. 'Shooter's running, third floor, dressed in black.'

'Affirmative,' came the reply.

I went to the gallery window and waited for the fireworks, and yeah, "fireworks" made for a pretty apt description. As I watched, the entire third floor of the car park flared up in a brilliant vermillion light threaded with molten cords of furious yellow fire.

A second or two passed before Stella spoke again. 'Threat neutralised,' she said, calm as you like.

Did I mention that Stella is a witch's familiar and a tough as nails spell-slinger? No? Well, here goes then. Three hags made Stella out of magic and spit over half a century ago – built themselves an enforcer to knock seven bells out of London's Uncanny bad guys. So far I'd say she's been doing a pretty bang-up job of it. She mostly looks after the big picture stuff around here—your higher-plane demonic entities, your cannibalistic death cults, your ancient curses—while I deal with the smaller jobs like missing persons and serial killers. It's not often our jobs intersect, but I'd lent her a hand on that nightmare realm gig, so she owed me this one and a couple more besides.

'Thanks, Stella,' I replied. 'You did us proud.'

I hung up the phone and let out a long sigh of relief. Eight insufferable weeks of tedium had finally paid off. All of that effort, all of that planning, and it was all done in a second. The killer was subdued and ready to be turned over and judged for his crimes. At least here on Earth. He'd have to wait until the day he passed to receive his eternal judgment, and as a multiple murderer, the die had already been cast on that one. His soul was destined for the Bad Place. No stating his case at the pearly gates, no passing Go, no collecting £200, the man was going to Hell in a handbasket.

I turned around to see Levant had taken off, leaving me alone among his collection. I walked over to the emoji mannequin and inspected the hole in its poop head. I could see the assassin's bullet embedded inside like a little silver nugget. It's funny; five minutes ago this piece of shit sculpture was unsold, but now the art world would be falling over themselves to get a hold of it. I shook my head. This whole scene was bonkers.

Still, what did I care? I'd put paid to a serial killer and avenged a slew of untimely ends. Thanks to me, the ghosts of a dozen victims would be able to cross over now, freed from the physical plane and released to their final reward. The job was done, the mission accomplished, now I could finally go home and make a dent in that pile of DVD boxed sets sat by the TV.

My phone rang. I was expecting it to be Stella, but the screen said otherwise. The incoming call was from DCI Stronge.

I picked up. 'I was just about to give you a bell, Kat. We got him.'

'Glad to hear it,' she replied, 'I'll send a couple of uniforms your way to get him processed.'

'You do that,' I said. 'In the meantime, I have a date with a stack of *Good Wife* DVDs.'

I was about to hang up, but Stronge wasn't done talking. 'Afraid that's going to have to wait.'

'Aw come on, what could possibly be more important than me finally watching the big Season 4 finale?'

A second of thought her end and then, 'Is that the one where Will gets shot?'

'What?' I screamed. 'Why would you do that?'

'Because you've got work to do, Fletcher. Now get yourself to the Heath, we just caught a new one.'

Bollocks.

2

My name is Jake Fletcher and I'm a P.I. The "P" can stand for whatever you like—"private", "paranormal", "platypus" for all I care—what matters is the job that goes with it. Without getting too bogged down in the details, I help my clients find their way to the spirit world. When a person dies a traumatic death their soul becomes detached and clings to its locality, trapped on the physical plane instead of riding the golden elevator to the great hereafter. I help those lost souls become un-marooned by solving their murders and bringing their killers to justice.

Why do I do what I do? Well, it's not to get rich, I can tell you that much. We ghosts aren't much concerned with the material things – which goes as much for money as it does anything else with a physical property. What use would money be to a spook anyway? What would I buy with the stuff? I mean, it's not like I need to bother watching Season 5 of *The Good Wife* anymore.

No, the reason I help out other ghosts is to offset some of my own bad mojo. See, back before I kicked the bucket I used to be an exorcist. You know the fellers: *"The power of*

Christ compels thee!" Crucifixes and holy water. Demonic possession. Children scrabbling about on the ceiling on all fours. All that malarkey. I also dealt with other supernatural nuisances, namely ghosts, or what we in the trade called "poltergeists". Clients would contact me to report a haunting and I'd swing by their property to cleanse it of spooks. Bish bash bosh. They'd get to sleep at night, I'd get paid. Everyone was happy. Well, almost everyone.

See, here's the rub... just like the rest of my exorcist peers, I used the same methods to send demons packing as I did ghosts. Unfortunately, as it turns out, exorcism is not a one-size-fits-all operation. Instead of sending those ghosts to their final reward—as I assumed I'd been doing—I had in fact been obliterating them. Wiping them off the map. Off *any* map.

It wasn't until I died and became a ghost myself that I realised the truth of it. I was a killer. A serial killer. Sure, I could claim I didn't understand the consequences of what I was doing, but there had to be a price to pay for rubbing out that many souls. It's why I busted out of the afterlife and ended up here a ghost; to avoid answering for my misdeeds. At first I was just running scared, but after I landed back on Earth, I decided I wanted to do something to make up for all those people I'd destroyed. To start saving souls the *right* way, and maybe, just maybe, save my own in the process.

As I made my way to Detective Stronge I wondered how much dirt I still had to scrape off my hide before I'd be clean. I arrived at Hampstead Heath at just gone one in the morning. A couple of uniforms flanked a ribbon of yellow police tape stretched across the park's western entrance, but I ghosted by them unseen.

In darkness, the black grass of the Heath stood revived, unfurling after another day spent crushed beneath the feet of footballers and dog walkers. The sounds of screaming children and picnickers had vanished with the dying light, leaving behind an eerie calm. Trees swayed against the charcoal sky, and leaves scurried to a gentle breeze that might have raised goosebumps were I able to feel its touch.

I followed the glare of floodlights and the flash of a distant camera across the West Heath to the scene of the crime. The area was attended to by a number of officers and forensics experts, plus constables from the Hampstead Heath Constabulary, whose K-9s had alerted them to the scene. I threaded through the officers invisibly to arrive at a border of tape marked DO NOT CROSS, positioned to ensure that the enclosed area was given a wide berth by anyone whose fat feet didn't belong there.

I phased through the cordon and saw the bodies. Two of them, both men, splashed across the grass like they were trying to catch moon tans. Their limbs were posed at awkward angles and their heads positioned in a way that told me they definitely weren't sleeping. The smaller of the two had a rock in his hand, which was covered in a crust of dried blood and matted hair. The back of the larger one's skull had been caved in like an egg shell, and one of his eyeballs hung from its socket, dislodged by the force of the blow. A river of congealed blood ran from each of his nostrils.

Turning to look past the police tape, I saw DCI Stronge. She sat alone on an aged oak bench beside Leg of Mutton Pond. She regarded me coolly as I made my way over and sat down beside her. Unlike the rest of her colleagues, Stronge possesses The Sight, which means she's able to see ghosts. She acquired it as the result of a run-in we had with a demonic entity known as a soul feaster. Sometimes, when a regular person is shown the world as it really is, their eyes open to the Uncanny and they become—and I'm sorry to keep throwing these terms your way—what we call an "Insider".

'What took you so long?' she asked, blowing on her coffee.

Stronge works in homicide and serious crimes, and was heading up this investigation. Tonight she wore her immaculate, flat-ironed hair in a neat bob that accentuated her angular cheekbones. The hair was brunette but her eyes were blue as the lights of the police cars I could see flashing in the distance.

'I was finishing up with Stella at the other place,' I told her.

'Your magic lady?' she snorted, shaking her head. 'Sorry to drag you back into the gutter.'

If I didn't know better I'd almost think she was jealous.

Ever since I got into the detective game, DCI Stronge had been invaluable to me. While Stella acts as my link to the realm of the Uncanny—one of them anyway—Stronge's my anchor to the regular world. My counterweight to balance out the crazy. She's also my go-between to the Metropolitan Police, which I work for in a clandestine, consultancy capacity.

'Where's your partner tonight?' I asked Stronge.

'He's on leave again after... well, you know.'

Our encounter with the soul feaster. The trauma he suffered back then caused what shrinks call a "dissociative fugue": a blackout coupled with severe amnesia that flares up like PTSD and requires regular psychiatric counselling. Although Maddox is none the wiser about what happened to him that day, his brain is still reeling from it. I can sympathise. The odd spell of absence is to be expected when you're dealing the fallout of a rampaging demon that skins people alive.

The Scene of Crime Officer approached in a white boiler suit and pulled down his face mask. 'The site's ready for inspection, ma'am,' he told Stronge.

'Let's go,' she replied, and followed him to the cordon with me tagging along unnoticed.

'I can take it from here, Officer,' she said, and off he went about his business, allowing Stronge and me to talk.

'Well, what do you think?' she asked.

I looked at the two bodies laying on the ground; at the rock wrapped in the stiff fingers of one, and at the cratered head of the other.

'Well,' I replied, 'I'm thinking it's probably not a suicide.'

Stronge harrumphed, took the last swig of her coffee and squeezed the paper cup flat. 'We're considering the possibility that it was a lover's quarrel.'

That figured. Even in the Grindr age, the West Heath was still a popular night-time cruising ground for gay men. The cops tolerated it so long as they cleaned up after themselves and kept it away from the kiddies.

'Could have been a spat,' I supposed. 'What do we know for sure?'

'Just two things. One: the victim is the only one with any wounds – the bludgeoner doesn't have a mark on him.'

'Could have been a heart attack. Sudden aneurism maybe.' I stroked my chin. 'What's the other thing?'

'The murderer, the man with the rock in his hand, forensics are telling me he's been dead for at least forty-eight hours.'

'Oh. Well, that's...'

'Yeah. It complicates things.'

The crime had to have occurred this evening, so how did

a two-day-old corpse wind up on the scene? My first thought was that someone must have bashed the one guy's head in and dumped the other body here hoping to fit him up for the murder, but Stronge soon disavowed me of that notion.

'Doesn't seem that way,' she said. 'The bone and brain fragments on the skinny guy are consistent with him perpetrating a close-quarters bludgeoning.'

'They couldn't have been sprinkled on after the fact?' I asked. *Sprinkled,* I said, like I was talking about decorating a cake.

'I know this is a bit out there,' supposed Stronge, 'but could the bludgeoner be a zombie? Assuming those are a thing.'

'They are,' I replied, 'but we don't see too many of them around here.'

No, this wasn't voodoo. Wrong continent. Wrong... vibe.

I looked to the bludgeoner's body and then back to Stronge. 'Notice anything else out of the ordinary?'

She considered the crime scene and narrowed her eyes. After a minute or so of contemplation, she admitted defeat. 'I don't see it.'

'Exactly,' I said. 'Where's the ghost?'

She slapped her forehead. 'Of course.' She was still relatively new to her gift—if you want to call being tuned into a world of phantoms and horrors a "gift"—and had yet to become used to seeing the world as it really was. 'So what are you thinking?' she asked. 'Another soul feaster?'

I swayed my head. 'I don't think so,' I said. 'Not this time.'

Call it a hunch, but something seemed different here. This was new, I was sure of it.

'Wait a second...' said Stronge, pointing to the two

bodies. 'You said "ghost" before. Shouldn't that be "ghosts," plural?'

'Not necessarily,' I argued.

Stronge was a brilliant detective, head and shoulders above me, but she still had a lot to learn about the paranormal.

I explained how not all traumatic deaths resulted in a disembodied spirit wandering the Earth. How a real villain's fate is decided before they die. Like I said before, the Devil claims his due with a bit more ferocity than the Man Upstairs. If someone's an undeniable piece of shit—I'm talking murderers, war criminals, *2 Broke Girls* fans—they get a one-way ticket to the Bad Place. No judgment in the afterlife, no paperwork to fill out, just a trapdoor to the fiery pit. I'm surprised I never got sent south for my crimes really. I can only imagine the Big Man wanted to get a proper, close-up look at me before he pulled the lever.

'Let's suppose the feller with the smashed skull was a bit naughty,' I said. 'A real baddie. That'd explain why he isn't around to say hello.'

'And what about the one with the rock?' asked Stronge. 'If you're saying he wasn't dragged to Hell, where did he get to?'

'You already told me his body's two days dead. That means he didn't die here. Which means his ghost could still be hanging about wherever it is that he *did* snuff it.'

Stronge bobbed her head. 'All right,' she said. 'That gives us something to run with.'

I bent down to get a better look at the two cadavers. The one with his eye hanging out looked to be in his mid-thirties and was a real lump of a bloke; a bald head, thick rhino neck and biceps like rugby balls. The scrawny one with the skull gavel in his hand couldn't have been older than twenty;

a mangy-looking thing dressed like a rough sleeper. Despite the chill, he was only wearing a t-shirt and had visible track marks up his left forearm. He also had a tattoo there that read, "What doesn't kill you only makes you stronger".

'Bit ironic,' I muttered.

'The big lad came with a wallet and driver's license,' said Stronge.

'The scag head?'

'Nothing.'

I nodded. It could never be easy, could it?

Stronge folded her arms. 'We should divvy up jobs. I'll check on one of their backgrounds while you look into the other.'

'So let me get this right,' I said, 'one of us has to rummage around the slums interviewing down-and-outs, while all the other has to do is run an ID through a computer?'

'That's right,' said Stronge, wearing the thinnest of smiles.

I'll give you two goes at guessing which job I got, but you'll only need the one.

3

It was left to me to find out who the kid with the ironic tattoo was, and how his two-day-old corpse wound up dumped on Hampstead Heath with a bloody rock in his paw and a sprinkling of brain bits.

Just like I always do when I'm in need of answers to tricky questions, I went to see Frosty, my man on the street. And that's "on the street" in the literal sense. Frosty's a rough sleeper too, or was at least before he froze to death begging one winter. These days he's a ghost, so he doesn't need sleep or loose change. Instead, he sits frozen to his final resting place, a patch of pavement next to an ATM opposite the square by Mornington Crescent station, draped by the shadow of Lord Cobden's statue. You'd think he'd get bored, sat there all day and night, but he manages to keep himself amused. He mainly succeeds in this by looking up the skirts of women waiting in line for the cashpoint, but sometimes he doles out titbits to chancers like me that come to him looking for local lore. For a price anyway.

'Evening, Frost,' I said as I appeared by his side.

He flinched at the sudden intrusion. I have that effect on

people. Since I'm able to arrive places instantly using my ghost powers, I often save myself the legwork of walking and translocate there instead. It's a real timesaver, but it does have a habit of upsetting folks who don't know I'm coming.

'What do you want, Fletcher?' Frosty growled.

As usual, he looked as though he'd spent a week trapped in a cold storage unit. Icicles clung to his whiskers and his skin had the pallor of old meat dipped in liquid nitrogen.

'Looking for an ID on a murder suspect,' I told him.

'Is that all?' he asked, then cleared his throat, rolled something around his gob and hawked it on the pavement next to my feet. 'What's in it for me?' he asked as the glob of ectoplasm rolled by my brogues.

Ever the charmer, old Frost.

I sighed and reached inside my jacket for his payment. His eyes lit up when he saw it: a can of Carlsberg Special Brew, the alcoholic's gut-rot of choice. Frosty doesn't have use for much in this world, but even in death, he was not without his vices.

'Give it 'ere,' he demanded, fingers twitching for his prize.

I keep a stock of the brew in reserve in case I'm ever in need of Frosty's services. Each tin is individually enchanted by my magician friend, Jazz Hands, a process that makes them tankable for ghosts. Without her blessing, Frosty wouldn't even be able to wrap a mitt around one, let alone enjoy its contents.

He snatched the can off me then pulled back the ring pull with a feculent fingernail to suck down the bruiser juice inside.

'Ready to do business?' I asked.

'Still feeling a bit cloudy,' he replied, feigning forgetfulness.

I sighed and handed him a second can, which he took in both hands like a squirrel with a nut.

'Not joining me?' he asked, popping it open.

'Thanks,' I said, 'but I'd sooner lick a stripper pole.'

He shrugged and knocked back the second can as quickly as the first. 'And a third on completion,' he told me.

'Fine,' I said.

Immediately, his attitude took a steep uptick. If he had a tail it would have been wagging.

'What can I do for you, my good man?' he asked, wiping his mouth with the back of a mittened hand.

I don't take pleasure in being Frosty's enabler, but since this is the only way I can get him to open his trap, he doesn't leave me much choice.

'Looking for a young feller,' I told him. 'Possible street kid.'

'Gonna need a bit more than that,' he replied.

'Early twenties. A user. Has a Nietzsche tattoo here,' I said, rolling up the sleeve of my jacket to show him the underside of my left forearm.

Frosty made a face like he'd just seen a hearse blow a tyre. 'Did it say, "What doesn't kill you can only make you stronger"?

'Yeah,' I replied, taken aback. 'Bloody hell, that was quick.'

It usually took Frosty a little while to cast out his feelers and get a handle on a person, but apparently, he'd nailed this one right out of the gate. Ordinarily, he gathers intel using something I can only describe as ghost ESP. Whereas I have a fairly ordinary complement of ghost powers—invisibility, intangibility, translocation—Frosty has something that's entirely his own. As if to make up for being rooted to the spot, he's able to know pretty much anything about his surroundings by reading the minds of those he comes in contact with, and given his permanent pitch by an ATM, that accounts for a whole lot of people. Even more impressively, he's able to read the minds of people his targets have been in contact with, which makes him something like the Oracle of Camden Town.

'Did you say he was a murder suspect?' Frosty asked, shocked. 'Ah, Fergal, what were ya thinking...?'

Now I had a name. 'You knew him personally?' I asked.

'Yeah. A runaway he was, fresh-faced thing when I met him a few years back. Came to town from Glasgow after a row with his folks.' Frosty shook his head. 'I told him to go back and make good with 'em before he got himself into trouble down 'ere. Looks like he didn't listen.'

It occurred to me that I hadn't mentioned Fergal was dead as well as in the frame for a murder, so I put it to Frosty as gently as I knew how.

He cast a sullen look to the ground. 'It's a rotten shame,' he said. 'A rotten shame. He was a good kid really.' His voice trailed slowly, like his words were unwilling to take flight.

'Sorry to hear that,' I said. I may not have a pulse, but I still have a heart. 'There's still a chance we can help him, though.'

'Help 'im 'ow? You said he'd done someone in. That's a one-way trip to the Bad Place, that is.'

'I said we were looking into the possibility that he'd done someone in,' I clarified. 'We don't know for sure if he did the deed.'

'Then ask his bleedin' ghost!' Frosty barked.

I explained that Fergal's phantom, if there was one, was likely at the location he'd bitten the dust a couple of days back. 'That's where I need to be looking,' I told Frosty. 'Except I haven't got a clue where to start. Maybe if I talk to someone who's spent time with him recently I'll learn something.'

'Sounds like a plan,' Frosty agreed.

'Right. So what can you tell me about Fergal's old...' I almost said "haunts," '...stomping grounds.'

'You'd wanna get yerself to South Ken,' he replied. 'Cardboard city in the disused Underground station there. That's where he used to bunk up.'

I nodded. 'Thanks,' I said. 'I can work with that.'

I reached into my jacket pocket for the last can of Special Brew.

Frosty waved it off. 'Keep it,' he sighed. 'I'm miserable enough without it.'

4

So long as I was determined to scurry around the bowels of Camden Town questioning vagrants, I was going to need a body. Don't get me wrong, being an apparition has its uses in the P.I. game, but when it comes to questioning witnesses, a set of lips is paramount. That's why I always keep a spare body on stand-by.

Another of my ghost powers, besides translocation, is being able to possess the living. It's funny, back when I was a breather there was a sign at my gym that used to say, "Take care of your body, it's the only one you get". True enough then, but a bag of shite now. My body's long gone, but that doesn't mean I can't borrow a rental from time to time.

It's not like I'm the only one at it. Ever found yourself spacing out and looking at your watch to find a half hour's vanished into thin air? Might be that you were the unwitting vessel of an invasive spirit. Of course, it's *far* likelier that you're just a bit of a ditz, so try not to fret about it. Very few ghosts are capable of possession, so chances are you've never personally been taken for a ride. Keep an eye out, though... you never know.

Me, I'm an expert at possession. A couple of seconds in the company of a living body and I'll have it dancing around like a marionette. That thing you call *you* is really just a container—a big old sack of blood, gristle, and bone—and I can edge you into the passenger seat like it was nothing. I'm not saying it's a nice thing to do to someone, taking ownership of their body against their will, which is why I try to make sure the people I possess are deserving of a bit of ill-treatment.

My go-to body belongs to a bloke called Mark Ryan. I've known him since high school, where he used to torment me on a daily basis. Mark's a City Boy now, the type that runs with the pinstripe suit crowd. When he's not managing hedge funds or chasing bimbos, he likes to go jogging in the most conspicuous places he can find, dressed in a pair of those five-toed sandals that only wankers wear. Mark is the kind of person who puts up a toilet roll with the paper hung underarm. I'm talking about a monster here.

Since I've used Mark as my meat suit so many times in the past, I have a psychic bead on him now. There's nowhere he can go that I won't find him, not that he's ever hiding. I always make sure to scrub any memories of our time together, so he has no clue I've been repeatedly hijacking his body for the better part of a decade.

Operating the pink blob of meat that Mark calls a brain, I marched him to a chicken shop back-alley that I'd read about online. I got the skinny from an urban explorer site on the dark web that told me there was an old ventilation shaft there that led into the tunnels – one that hadn't been capped off like the rest. The people living below used it to snatch supplies from the surface, dragging bits of refuse to the depths that they fashioned into their jerry-rigged shantytown.

It was getting on for three in the morning when I reached the alleyway, well past pub chucking-out time, when the streets of London were as quiet as they ever got. Checking the coast was clear, I ducked into the alley, located the unfastened ventilation fan, and pried it back to sneak into the shaft beyond. Down a grimy passageway I crept, hopscotching piles of reeking rubbish and stagnant puddles of God-knows-what. Following the instructions I'd found online, I pursued an old emergency escape route to a flight of stairs, which I carefully descended to reach the station's crumbling train platform. Stepping on to the southbound track, I tiptoed over a steroidal rat and headed off into the tunnel's perpetual darkness.

I used the beam of a Maglite torch to make sure I steered clear of the main rail, which I'd heard the tunnel's inhabitants leeched electricity from to power their second-hand TV sets and hot plates. Despite being inhabited, South Kentish Town is known as a ghost station, and with good reason. Anguished howls echoed down the tunnels, bouncing from arched brick walls coated with spray-can art reminiscent of primitive cave drawings. Sinister stick figures danced beside illiterate, doom-laden proclamations, meant to ward off intruders. It was spooky as shit down there, and that's coming from a bona fide dead man riding around in a suit of haunted meat.

I passed by the warnings and pressed on through a rubble-strewn no-man's land to arrive at a cluster of shacks made from lumber and cardboard. The air was thick and heavy, and I felt eyes crawling over me as I passed along the shanty town's thoroughfare. I saw a couple of raggedy men crouching by a fire, roasting a rat on a spit, and thought back to an Attenborough documentary I'd seen about an ecosystem living at the bottom of the Atlantic ocean. Giant worms, thriving somehow in the poisonous warmth of volcanic vents. I saw the same thing in the eyes of these men, a Darwinian drive to endure even this most hostile of environments. To survive, no matter the odds.

A figure stepped from a doorway as I passed by his makeshift shack. 'Clear off, ya fooker,' he barked.

Not exactly the reception I'd been hoping for, but it was a start.

I didn't want to dazzle the man, so I kept the beam of my torch pointed at the ground as he shuffled from the gloom. As he drew closer I got a look at his face, lit by the flames of the nearby fire. His pallid skin was charcoal-smudged, his features decorated with a single, milky eye.

I held up my hands in surrender. 'Don't mean to bother you, feller,' I said. 'Just looking for some info on a kid who used to live around here. Went by the name of Fergal.'

I saw now that the disgruntled resident had brought a friend with him; a malnourished rottweiler on a threadbare length of twine.

'And 'oo are you to be askin'?' the man demanded.

'A friend.'

'A fookin' queer are ya?'

Not the most enlightened outlook I'll admit, but given the bloke's circumstances, I was ready to let that one slide. 'I'm not looking for a dust-up,' I told him, 'so why don't you go back to your hut and let me get on?'

'Why don't *you* get ta fook?' he enquired.

His dog growled and strained at the bit of string wrapped around its neck.

'Let's put a pin in that for now, shall we?' I suggested.

He leered at me, exposing a set of teeth like the tombstones of a half-demolished graveyard. 'That's a fancy suit yer wearin'. Did it come with a fancy wallet?'

I stood my ground. 'So long as you're willing to talk, we can do a deal.'

'Ahm not here ta deal,' he explained. 'Ahm here to take yer fookin' money.'

I sized him up. Without the pooch he was nothing to get in a tizz about—more skeleton than man, really—but that dog of his definitely looked hungry.

'You sure you wanna do this, mate?' I asked.

Whether I was bluffing or giving him one last chance was hard to say. Either way, the outcome was not the one I desired.

'Sic 'im, Tyson!' the tramp yelled, setting the rottweiler free.

The dog's hair stood up along the ridge of its spine and it came at me, jaw snapping and foaming at the muzzle. I was hoping to get an arm around its neck as it leapt at me; instead, I got its teeth in my wrist.

I screamed as the dog's fangs sunk into the flesh of Mark's forearm, sending a jolt of pain straight to the brain I was borrowing. I took a quick inventory of my situation and arrived at the following course of action: *"If in doubt, give it a clout"*. I raised my Maglite and thumped the dog on the top of its head as hard as I could muster.

Crack.

The torch shattered to bits.

The dog yelped but remained firmly attached. I balled a fist and landed a punch, but the dog refused to budge.

I'd need to employ a change of tack quickly before the fanged bastard managed to chew through to an artery. My punches were doing nothing to penetrate its thick skull, and besides, I didn't want to be bashing the thing over the head. I knew it wasn't really a bastard, it was just hungry and poorly-treated, a victim of circumstance really. I know, I know, I'm a real bleeding heart. Well... bleeding arm in this case.

Just then I landed on an idea.

What if I could possess the dog and get it off me that way? I'd never tried taking the reins of an animal brain before, but how hard could it be?

Very hard indeed, as it turns out.

I allowed my spirit to drift out of Mark's body so I could take control of the rottweiler, but when I got there I felt an immediate sense of unsteadiness. With a dog's brain, the toeholds I usually relied on just weren't available. It's like I was working with a sheer wall, with nothing there to grip. I clawed at the surface, desperate to find purchase, but it was no good.

I was falling...

Falling...

And then I found it.

A crack, just wide enough for me to get the tips of my fingers inside. Just wide enough for me to anchor on to.

I shot out a hand and latched to the chink in the wall.

Having slowed my descent, I took a metaphorical breath and steadied myself. Ready to resume my attack, I pressed my forehead against the cold surface of the wall and felt my will grind up against the dog's own. I tried to force my way in—to wrest control of its psyche—but the beast was strong. Much stronger than I'd expected. Even after I'd managed to slip through the first line of its defences, dominion remained well out of reach. The mutt was a thousand times harder to possess than Mark was, which spoke poorly of his mental fortitude.

I did manage to obtain some level of control, though, even if it was only fleeting. Instead of forcing the dog's psyche into the passenger seat, our minds merged, filling my consciousness with thoughts of chewed-up tennis balls, walks in the park, and furiously humped legs. In return, I sent the dog some thoughts of my own, chief of which was, *"Let go of my arm right now and attack the fucker with the milky eye"*.

I wish you could have seen the face of the cackling dosser when his loyal attack hound unlatched from my arm, snarled like a timber wolf and went tearing off in his direction. If that didn't delight you, you'd definitely have enjoyed the face he made when the starving dog got a big, wet bite of his ball bags.

I know I did.

With that message sent, I hit the ejector seat and returned to Mark's body as the man and his mutt went scarpering off in different directions, their friendship brought to a sudden and unexpected close.

The fracas with the dog had only lasted a few seconds, which meant Mark hadn't been up to do much in the meantime besides scrabbling around in the dust, babbling on and on about losing his mind. Classic Mark.

I hopped back inside and inspected his wounded arm. It was a mess for sure, but he'd live – a bit of iodine on it and he'd be right as rain. Besides, I had bigger things to worry about in that moment, starting with the disconcerting taste of tramp dick I'd been left with since my human/canine mind merge.

As I sat there, scraping at my tongue with the rough fabric of my sleeve, I heard footsteps coming my way. I went to find out who it was with my torch, but it lay in pieces at my feet. Determined not to be snuck up on, I span around, ready to take on my next attacker, whoever they might be.

'Who wants some now?' I shouted, fists raised. 'Come on then, let's be 'avin' ya!'

From the darkness stepped a young woman wearing a coat so big it made the tiny hands that stuck out of its sleeves look like a pair of bell clappers.

'I brought you a bandage,' she said, holding up a surprisingly clean-looking rag. 'For your arm.'

The young woman approached carefully. She was only a slip of a thing, and had the kind of eyes that belonged on a puppy dog. 'I knew him,' she said as she patched up my punctured wrist. 'Fergal I mean. Is he all right?'

My face told her all she needed to know. 'He was a nice guy,' she sighed. 'Hard to come by down here. Most of the blokes who end up this way are scum. He was sweet, though. Never tried anything on.'

That's two character witnesses who spoke well of Fergal now. It was getting to look increasingly unlikely that he'd been dragged off to Hell.

'When did you see Fergal last?' I asked her.

'A couple of nights ago,' she replied. 'When he OD'ed down here and I had to call him an ambulance.'

'How did you manage that?' I asked. I could see the tunnel-dwellers had tapped the rail line for leccy, but it was hard to imagine getting a five-bar signal down here.

'I went up top and used a payphone to call 999,' she explained. 'Led the paramedics down here myself. Last I saw of Fergal was when the two of them carried him off on a stretcher.'

Okay, looked like I had a decent lead to follow. Time to visit the nearest hospital. 'Thanks,' I said. 'For the info and for patching me up.'

I opened Mark's wallet and handed her the contents, but as I turned to leave she reached out, touching my arm to stop me.

'There was something a bit... wrong, though,' she said.

'The paramedics. They had all the right gear and everything but they looked... weird.'

'Weird how?' I asked.

'Pale. Strung out. Jittery. Like they needed a fix of something.'

'What are you saying?'

'I'm saying they looked as much like junkies as the rest of us.'

Jittery junkie paramedics, eh? Now there was a wrinkle in the story.

5
———

The generally accepted etymology of the word "gumshoe" describes a detective dressed in rubber-soled galoshes that enable him to creep up stealthily on thieves and wrongdoers. In reality, the trade doesn't involve that much excitement. Most of the time, being a P.I. involves endless stakeouts and chasing leads no matter how futile they might seem, which means pounding the streets, day in day out, until the soles of your shoes are worn thin and covered in chewing gum. That's what the word "gumshoe" means to me anyway. Hard graft and low reward.

Locating Fergal's ghost had proved a challenge so far, but now I had a plan. Using GMaps on my enchanted mobile phone, I plotted the quickest route to the nearest hospital and walked the journey there. In all likelihood, he'd died in the emergency room, but if he'd perished in the ambulance along the way, there was a chance his spirit had become dislocated and left by the roadside. By following the ambulance's route on foot, I'd be sure not to miss him either way.

Having emerged blinking into the light of the back-alley,

I plotted my course and made off. As I walked, I tilted Mark's head to the sky and looked out to the smog-streaked horizon. A new day had dawned. I hadn't realised I'd been below ground for that long, but then it's easy to lose track of things when you don't abide by the usual time markers like mealtimes and bedtimes. Being a ghost, I don't need food or sleep, so the days often merge into one. It doesn't help that daybreak in a polluted city like London is less of a glorious, peachy sunrise than a slow, murky bleed from black to grey.

I'd been walking for about an hour when I heard a commotion up ahead. Carving a rut into the pavement was a young man, pacing up and down and wailing at passers-by. Despite his cries for assistance he remained invisible and unheard. Hurt yet neglected. Of course, in this city that could account for just about anyone in need of help. This was different, though. This man was beyond help. This man was dead.

The ghost of Fergal span in circles, throwing his arms around the commuters strolling by him but passing through them as though he were made of smoke.

'Easy,' I told him, holding my open palms out to placate him.

'You can see me?' he screeched.

I'm lucky I got to him in time. Fergal hadn't been out there long, but from the looks of things, he was already beginning to turn feral. That's what happens to some ghosts —to most ghosts in fact—sooner or later they lose their marbles and become full-blooded, chain-rattling spooks. Whether it's the loneliness or the shock of dying I don't really know, but it's as though a semblance of their physical form remains while their mind dissolves away, turning them from a rational person into a screaming, ghost train phantom. I've seen it happen too many times, which is why I decided to become a paranormal P.I. – so I could help folks pass over before they turned into malevolent spirits. That and to plug some landfill into the smoking crater I'd made of my soul.

I told Fergal to calm down and follow me to a side street. I was inside Mark still, and didn't want to look like a lunatic talking to himself in public. Fergal pursued me, practically nipping at my heels. He was wild and twitching and so frail that he looked as though he had the metabolism of a hummingbird, except that he had no metabolism at all. Not anymore.

'What's happening to me?' he begged.

I hate this part. Hate that it falls on me to tell a person they've died, but I make it my job all the same. Mostly I do it because I remember how it was when I croaked. I didn't have anyone holding my hand. No one told me the rules, I had to figure the ghost thing out myself. Yeah, I already knew a few things from my time as an exorcist, but there were still an awful lot of blanks to fill.

It hurts being dead. It's not an easy transition, going from being a living breathing person to a spooky hologram. People say break-ups and bereavements are hard, but they should try snuffing it. The only reason that one doesn't make the list is because no one's writing about it, but take it from me, dying is the worst.

I let Fergal down as easy as I knew how. I have a bit of boilerplate I use to bring new ghosts up to speed and let them know how things work down here. I explain how they're stuck between worlds like a penny in a sofa, but that they can still cross to the other side, just so long as they help me finish up their business on Earth. To that end, I disclosed to Fergal how his body had been found on Hampstead Heath with a murder weapon in its hand.

He was shocked to say the least.

'Any idea how you wound up there?' I asked.

'Not a clue,' he replied. 'I nodded off underground and the next thing I knew I found myself up here.'

That seemed to confirm my suspicion that he'd died en route to the hospital, but not how his body had arrived on the Heath two days later.

'Why do you want to help me anyway?' he asked, lip curled. 'What's in it for you?'

I could understand the suspicion. Living on the streets makes a man tough – it's no wonder Fergal wasn't too trusting of a stranger offering free salvation, particularly when he dressed like a door-to-door salesman.

'The truth is, saving your arse is as much for me as it is for you,' I told him. 'I made some mistakes when I was still among the living, and helping you out offsets some of that. That's how it works: your wayward soul goes to the Great Beyond and I earn some Brownie points for my trouble. Win-win.'

'So you're sort of like a... spirit guide?'

'If you like, yeah, but not in the dreamcatcher, crunchy granola, beat poetry sense.'

A sudden thought crossed Fergal's mind. 'Do my mum and dad know that I'm... you know...?'

'I'll make sure the police pass on the message,' I told him, and he nodded grimly.

That could be Stronge's job – payback for giving me this shitty little number.

Before I left, I asked Fergal if he knew anything else. Anything at all about how he wound up a suspect in a murder case. Did he have any enemies? Anyone looking to do him harm? Anyone he wanted to do harm to? All my questions met with a big, fat nothing.

I was going to have to look for clues elsewhere.

I had planned on going to the hospital to ask some questions about those two paramedics, but DCI Stronge had other ideas. I was told to meet her at St. Pancras Mortuary and to come alone, which was code for, "Leave the meat suit at home".

Not a problem. Mark was about to reject me anyway, so the sooner I cut him loose the better. I can stay inside a living body for a while, but I always get the boot in the end. A body isn't made for two souls, that's just the way it is. I can squat in one for a time, but sooner or later I get my eviction notice and have to toddle on. After that it's hours, sometimes days before I can set up shop again. Don't ask me why it works that way, I don't write the rules.

I dropped Mark off at his apartment, an upscale bachelor pad near Regent's Park with a dedicated beer cooler in the kitchen and a lounge decked out with a speaker system powerful enough to loosen bowels. I sat Mark down on his oversized sofa and went to work scrubbing the events of the last few hours from his mind.

Mark's never been too strong between the ears, to the extent that I'm now able to not only format his memories, but to replace them with new ones. It's a skill I've developed to make my possessions a bit kinder on the lad. I'd been getting a fair bit of use out of him lately, and the recurring gaps in his memory were making him anxious. He'd gone to his therapist about it and been referred to a doctor, but the PET scans they gave him showed nothing abnormal. Still, Mark was convinced he had something wrong with him. He was worrying so much about a non-existent brain tumour that he was going to give himself a very real stomach ulcer. So, being the very milk of human kindness, I figured out a way to fill the potholes I'd been leaving in the poor bugger's head.

Thanks to my jiggery-pokery, when Mark replays the events of the last few hours, instead of seeing himself getting into a fight with a derelict's attack dog, he'll remain convinced that he stayed in and binge-watched three seasons of *Entourage* (I wanted to go with something classy like *The Wire*, but the memories I create have to be halfway realistic for them to stick). Oh, and as for the bandaged wound on his wrist, he got that when he was slicing a block of artisanal Parmesan and the grater slipped. Not a great deception I realise, but the best I could come up with in a hurry.

It's ironic, Mark ending up with a wounded wrist, seeing as he once gave me one of my own. It was a long time ago, back when we were in Year Nine. He'd managed to lay his hands on a pair of handcuffs and used them to manacle me to a classroom radiator. It was a shitty thing to do, but the humiliation was only half of it. While the teacher was out of the room, Mark and his dickhead friends stood around laughing as the handcuffs heated up, until they finally got so hot that the one attached to my wrist cooked me. Even though I don't have a working nose, I can still smell the burnt hair. The sizzling meat.

Any other kid would have been expelled for doing something like that, but Mark's dad was a big deal round our way—a lawyer with a lot of money and a lot of clout—and he made sure the headteacher saw things his way. Whether he paid him off or threatened him legally I don't know, but it was decided that a stain on his son's record at such an early age could wreck a promising future career, so Mark was allowed to carry on at the school unpunished.

I want you to remember that any time you question the ethics of me borrowing another man's body. Since I died I've done everything in my power to walk the path of the righteous, but Mark Ryan... Mark Ryan deserves all that he has coming to him and then some.

Anyway, enough of the boo-hoo, and back to the job at hand. As instructed, I met Stronge at the mortuary, where an examination of the cadavers found on Hampstead Heath was taking place. The two bodies had been laid out side-by-side. The slab on the left bore the weight of the rhino-necked victim with the cratered head and the dangling eyeball, while the other was draped by Fergal's gaunt, pockmarked frame. Each of the bodies had a small piece of printed card tied to its toe by a bit of string, which made them look like morbid Christmas tree presents, gift tagged to God.

I stood to one side and observed while the resident mortician, Dr Anand, inspected the corpses and related her findings to Stronge. It always felt strange, the three of us being together in that room, mainly because the first time it happened, I was looking down at my own dead body, scattered across a ceramic slab in four big chunks. It wasn't an experience I'd recommend, in case you were wondering.

Dr Anand was excellent at what she did. Nothing slipped by her. She was smart, capable and dependable; as true blue as the ultramarine apron she wore to keep blood spatter from her hospital whites. Which is not to say she was all sweetness and light. Anand enjoyed a gallows humour considered distasteful even by her peers. I once heard a story about her time as a medical resident working the graveyard shift at the Royal London Hospital. The story went that her and a group of fellow residents had ordered a 2 a.m. pizza, only for the delivery boy to wind up delivered himself, on a gurney. He'd been involved in a serious collision on the way to the hospital, a real axle-plaiter. When the surgeons failed to revive the boy, she was reported to have shrugged and asked, "So what happened to our pizza?"

As Doctor Anand went about her work, entirely unaware of my presence, I examined the toe tags on the bodies. Neither had a name on it, just case numbers, which meant the police were still chasing an ID on the big feller. Stronge must have thought she was quids in when she pulled the licence from his wallet, but I guess it had turned out to be bogus.

'TBI,' said Anand, suddenly.

'What's that?' asked Stronge, who'd spaced out after another fifteen-hour shift.

'Popeye here,' replied Anand, aiming a finger at the corpse with the dislodged eyeball. 'Cause of death: Traumatic Brain Injury. Lethal blunt force injury to the parietal lobe.'

'I see,' said Stronge. 'And is the injury consistent with the rock that came in with the other body?'

'I can't say for certain without further examination,' Anand replied, 'but I'll bet you a bag of chips it is.'

Stronge nodded. 'And what about the other one?'

Anand made a whistling sound like a car mechanic about to deliver a devastating repair fee. 'Again, I'll need a bit more time to get into the hows of it, but I can give you my cursory findings. There are three things that stand out right away. First of all, the genitals have been mutilated, but that's really just a side note.'

I stole a look. I hadn't been checking hard enough the first time, but now I inspected Fergal's body properly, I could see that his old chap had taken a bit of a blow, and not in a good way. From the looks of things, the tip had been removed, leaving him with little more than a stump. It was an old wound, though, and well-healed.

'As you can see,' Anand went on, 'the mutilation occurred some time ago and has already been treated surgically.'

Stronge nodded. 'I can see that. So what's the second *of all*?'

'I found heavy post-mortem bruising on the cadaver's right hand. Most likely caused by the murder weapon as it ricocheted off the victim's skull.'

If the bruising really had happened after Fergal died, which all signs pointed to, someone had gone to some major lengths to frame him.

'You mentioned a third thing,' said Stronge.

'I did,' replied Anand, 'And I saved the best till last.' She paused for effect. 'From what I can tell, the body's been exsanguinated.'

Stronge sighed. 'Let's pretend for a second like I don't know what that word means.'

But I knew what it meant.

It meant sucked dry of blood.

It meant vampires.

6

Here's what vampires aren't:

Adolescent dreamboats with devastating cheekbones and pallid skin that sparkles in the sunlight.

Sophisticated gentlemen dressed in top hats and tails who sup delicately on lusty young virgins.

Brooding teenage girls with dairy heifer eyes and needle-sharp fangs who leave their victims with nothing more challenging than a light headache.

So what are they really?

Parasites.

Killers.

Bloodsucking freaks with an unquenchable thirst for the old Type O.

From the looks of things, these vamps were smarter than the average, though. They were posing as night shift paramedics, rolling around town after sunset, picking up donors and carting them off in their mobile blood bank. They were careful enough to only prey on people who wouldn't be missed too, which told me they definitely had a couple of brain cells to rub together. No, these weren't your regular sun-dodgers. If I was going to go at these two, I'd need to go prepared.

While Stronge followed some leads on Popeye the Bludgeoned Man, I continued to work the dead junkie angle. Since I stepped up my caseload from regular homicides to things of a more supernatural nature, vampire paramedics were right in my wheelhouse. I had to be careful, though. When it came to bloodsuckers I only knew the basics. I needed to discuss the matter with someone a little more knowledgeable on the subject, which is how I ended up paying a visit to my old friend, Jazz Hands.

Jazz owns a dilapidated magic shop tucked down a King's Cross back street. The shop's called Legerdomain, a clever little pun that she must have dreamed up back when she had a sense of humour. As I entered—still in my ghost form—a bell tinkled; an early warning system Jazz had installed to alert her of any uninvited paranormal visitors. The shop was full, as ever, of alluring little objects: things that vanished, things that appeared from nowhere, things that floated in thin air. All of them stage tricks. The real magic was kept strictly behind locked doors, away from prying eyes.

'What is it now?' asked Jazz Hands, peering at me across the counter through a pair of violet-lensed glasses.

She'd fashioned the specs herself to be able to see phantoms, or more accurately, to see me. As far as I knew, I was the only ghost who ever dropped by. The only person who visited the shop *at all* according to the thick layer of dust that blanketed the place.

'I came to pick your brains,' I told her. A bad turn of

phrase, now I thought about it, remembering the smashed-up skull back at the morgue.

'I see,' Jazz Hands replied, fussing at a loose thread on her sleeve. Today, like most days, she wore a grungy, moth-eaten jumper and a folksy scarf that tethered her cloud of frizzy auburn hair to the rest of her head. 'And which denizens of the underworld do you plan on doing battle with this week?' she asked. 'Werewolves? Abominable snowmen? Creatures from the Black Lagoon?'

Jazz wasn't too thrilled about what I did for a living, but I had her over a barrel on the matter. On one hand, it filled her with maternal dread whenever I pitted myself against the supernatural and risked what little life I had. On the other, she didn't want me going to the Bad Place when I inevitably did end up answering to the Big Man, and the only way I was buying my way out of that was by playing boy scout. Pure thoughts and good deeds, those were my tickets to paradise, and Jazz Hands knew it. Didn't mean she had to like it, though, and I could understand the dirty feeling it gave her. In many ways, she was as much an enabler to me as I was to old Frosty.

I explained the situation with the vampires and how I was trying to chase them down. 'Before they can bleed anyone else dry,' I added for effect.

'I don't understand,' she replied. 'You say the victim was drained in an ambulance, but that his body was found on Hampstead Heath next to another corpse?'

'That's right.'

'But why?'

'I don't know for sure, but I'm guessing the vamps bashed the big guy's head in and dumped Fergal's body to cover up their part in the murder.'

'Hm. Why would vampires clever enough to employ a

mobile blood bank think the police too stupid to determine a body's actual time of death? And besides, so long as the vampires were draining one corpse dry, why leave a second one full of blood?'

She was right, something didn't fit. My brain tied up in a knot thinking about it. I'd just gotten going on this case but it was already starting to look like a 500 piece puzzle. 'You've got a point,' I admitted, 'I don't have all the answers. I reckon I know where I can get them, though...'

'If you're thinking what I think you're thinking—'

'It's gotta be done, Jazzer. I've gotta Van Helsing this shit.'

'You can't be serious? Taking on two vampires? Vampires are undead, Fletcher, which means they can hurt other undead, including ghosts.'

'It's the only way Fergal gets his wings. Otherwise, he's stuck here forever.'

'You have no idea how powerful these creatures can be.'

'Then tell me. Help me know what I'm going up against.'

Jazz Hands' eyes betrayed a complicated cocktail of emotions: pity, dread, devotion, but mostly just plain aggravation. Eventually, she reached under the shop counter and came back with a loosely-stitched tome stamped with the words "Codexul Vampir."

'A vampire's power is determined by a variety of factors,' she explained, 'but mainly their age and bloodline.' She consulted an index, then carefully peeled back the book's pages to arrive at a fragile sheet of parchment that looked as though it were made of animal skin. 'Here,' she went on, pointing to some chicken scratch written in a language I didn't comprehend. 'A list of powers that have been attributed to nosferatu over the centuries...'

She ran through a menu of potential traits—immortality, night vision, superhuman strength, hypnotism, bites that caused paralysis, the ability to turn into a cloud of gas—the list went on and on. A much shorter list described their known weaknesses, which amounted to little more than an allergy to silver, an intolerance to sunlight, and, for reasons quite beyond my grasp, a tremendous fear of antique clocks.

'What about wooden stakes through the heart?' I asked.

Jazz looked me up and down, judging me by a set of standards I could only guess at. 'Show me one creature that *does* respond favourably to having a stake hammered through its heart.'

Fair point.

'In any case,' she went on, 'given a vampire's vulnerability to the light of day, you'd be much better off armed with one of these…'

Making a rare trip from her stool, she went to the framed picture of paranormal debunker James Randi that hung behind the shop counter. Unfastening a hidden catch, she swung the picture aside on an invisible hinge to access the wall safe beyond. Turning her back on me to conceal the strong box's combination—as well as its contents—she delved inside and removed a ceramic sphere about the size of a tennis ball. She set it down gently on the shop counter and I squatted to get a look at it. It reminded me of a Christmas bauble.

'Go on then, what is it?' I asked.

Her eyes took on a smug twinkle. 'In laymen's terms, bottled sunlight,' she said, folding her arms like a genie granting a wish.

'Is that all?' I replied, feigning disregard. Jazz Hands was an easy wind-up, and it always tickled me to tweak her foibles.

She placed her palms on the counter and leaned across to me. 'Do you have any idea of the skill and patience required to produce a magical grenade capable of emitting enough UV light to destroy a vampire?' she asked.

'I dunno,' I said with a shrug, 'not that much I'm guessing.'

'"*Not that much*"?' she screeched. 'You ungrateful little shit! When I think of all the work I put in on your behalf! The hours! The back-breaking toil!'

I held up my hands. 'Whoa, Jazz, you are easier to play than a wind-up music box.'

She gave me the evil eyes over her glasses. 'Let us return to the matter at hand. These vampires of yours... I expect you'd like to know where to find them?'

'Yes, please,' I replied demurely.

'I see. Well, when it comes to setting up a den, vampires tend to look for somewhere secure from light. Somewhere underground usually, most likely a cellar. They tend to cluster as well, so if it's two vampires working together, chances are they're cohabiting.'

'Okay, that narrows it down some. So what should I do to find them?' I asked, thinking out loud. 'Check property listings within a set perimeter of their feeding territory, zoning in on homes with basements? Go to The Beehive and ruffle some feathers? Find another vampire in their clan and put the squeeze on them?'

'You could do those things,' she replied. 'Or you could go to the hospital they work at and get an address from their records.'

'Right. Or that. I mean, if you want to go the obvious route.'

Jazz smirked.

'Wait, they're not just going to hand that information out, are they? What about data protection?'

'What about it?' she replied. 'Is obtaining private records

going to be any more difficult than knocking on every house in Camden that has a basement and hoping a vampire answers the door?'

Fair point.

I took the UV grenade from the counter and placed it carefully in the pocket of my jacket.

'Take two,' she said, removing another from the wall safe. 'Just promise me one thing.'

'Yes, yes, I promise my arse is every bit as tight and toned as you've heard.'

'Find the vampire den,' she said, ignoring me, 'but don't go walking in there alone. If you absolutely have to go inside, make sure Stella Familiar goes in with you. This is what the London Coven built her for. Don't be a hero.'

'Yes, mother,' I sighed, taking the hand grenade off her.

7

I was hoping not to need Mark again so soon, but a job's a job.

The next stage of my investigation—finding the vampire den—would call upon all my powers of persuasion, and though I do consider myself a man of no small charm, I'd need Mark's good looks to really seal the deal. My natural charisma coupled with his genetic makeup makes for a pretty unbeatable combination. Don't get me wrong, I'm easy on the eye, but Mark has the kind of classic, chiselled looks you rarely see outside of that filthy rich, country club set. Plus he has a flesh and blood body that your everyday person is able to actually see, which chicks seem to like.

When I homed in on Mark I found him sat in a chair getting an eighty quid haircut from a late-night barber. It was one of those swanky, hipster places where all the staff wear waxed moustaches and sailor tattoos they haven't earned. In other words, a typical Mark establishment. The salon was packed, every chair filled, but neither the stylists or customers could see me. To them, I was as invisible as a homeless ninja.

I glided up behind Mark and prepared to make him my soul mule when a sudden flash of light bounced off the mirror in front of me. I turned over my shoulder to see a slim black man dressed in a long white coat and a matching wide-brimmed hat. At first, I took him for a ghost, but no, he was something else. Something very *else*. The black man in white was wreathed in a divine light and emanated a faint gospel music, like a distant choir. The guy absolutely *hummed* with the Uncanny.

'Mister Fletcher?' he purred.

The voice sounded familiar but I couldn't quite place it. 'Who's asking?' I replied.

'My name is Adonael,' he explained. 'Angel and celestial attendant of God.'

'Sorry, sunshine,' I replied. 'Still none the wiser.'

He placed a hand on his heart in mock consternation. 'You really don't remember me? I have to say I'm disappointed, I rather thought I'd made an impression upon you.' He cleared his throat, and when he spoke again he did so in the voice of the actress, Whoopi Goldberg. *'You drifted from the light, Jake. You revolted against God.'* He smiled and returned to his usual masculine, if still a bit effeminate, purr. 'Remember me now?'

'So you're the Big Man's stooge, are you? The one who spoke to me through my *Ghost* DVD?'

Yeah, it's a long story. Needless to say, I'd dealt with the bloke before, but never face to face. I didn't really know much about him except that he'd been given the job of keeping tabs on yours truly. The rest was all hypothesis, but if I had to hazard a guess I'd say he was some low-level, letter of the law, paid on commission, apple-polishing jobsworth of an angel.

He frowned and hooked his thumbs into the belt of his

coat. 'Take your last look at London, Mister Fletcher,' he said. 'You're coming with me now.'

'I very much fucking doubt that.'

His face contorted into a scowl. 'I have been duly sanctioned by the Almighty to retrieve you from this earthly plane and transport your soul to the afterlife, where you will be judged for your mortal—and now immortal—sins.'

'What are you banging on about?' I asked. 'I'm already off the naughty step, you told me so yourself. I sent a soul feaster packing, and if that wasn't enough to put me in the clear I helped banish a nightmare demon, and now—if you'll get out of the way and let me do my job—I'm going to nip a couple of vampires in the bud. I'm not saying my account's in the black just yet, mate, but it must be near as.'

'You are a long way from having a clean slate, Mister Fletcher. A very long way indeed.'

What was this? Crossed wires? Some administrator upstairs putting my name on the wrong form? What had I done wrong to have this traffic warden writing me up a ticket?

'So what is it then? What's got you so hot and bothered that you decided to come down here and stake out my meat suit?' I spat, pointing to Mark, who sat oblivious in the barber chair getting his hair cut into something out of a GQ magazine.

'You destroyed a heavenly relic,' the angel replied. 'The seraphim sword.'

Oh right, that thing. During my run-in with the soul feaster, I'd kind of let it get burned up by witch fire. It was an honest mistake; the kind that happens to the best of us.

'Are you having me on? That was ages back. Let it go, mate.'

'The seraphim sword was an invaluable weapon in our

eternal fight against the forces of evil,' said the angel. 'It was ancient and irreplaceable, and you are to be held accountable for its loss.'

'It was an accident!' I explained. 'An accident that happened while I was saving a bunch of people from getting murdered.'

'Rules are rules,' he scolded, curtly.

I was right. The man in white fancied himself a bounty hunter, but he was really just a pious bureaucrat. An errand boy. Yet another thorn in my dead arse.

'Isn't this all a bit petty?' I said. 'I thought you'd be above all that, what with being an angel. Well, I mean, you *say* you're an angel...'

'I am an angel.'

'Then where's your harp?'

'My harp?' he sputtered. 'Where do you think you are, Mister Fletcher, Sunday School? Angels don't wear gowns and frolic in the clouds, and God isn't some old man with a white beard sitting on a throne.'

'So he is a man?'

I felt pretty sure that information wasn't meant for my ears.

The angel went silent, realising he'd been caught talking out of school, then decided he didn't care. 'You'll find out soon enough,' he told me, and unlatched a set of glowing manacles from his belt.

Now, I don't take too kindly to handcuffs. Haven't done since the day the toolbag sat next to me getting his barnet done chained me to a red-hot radiator. Besides, there was no way I was having this little Hitler getting paid commission for banging me up.

'Sorry, pal,' I told him. 'Looks like you're going home empty-handed.'

I went to give the angel the old Irish goodbye, but when I tried to teleport, nothing happened. I looked in the wall mirror and tried again, but instead of vanishing, I came apart like a couple of misaligned transparencies and snapped back together again.

'I'm afraid that's not going to work,' said the man in white. 'Now kindly put on the cuffs before I'm forced to do so myself.'

"Not bloody likely," I thought, and said, now I come to think of it.

'Catch me if you can,' I told him.

I leapt into the customer to my right—a twenty-something getting his man bun trimmed—and took possession of his body.

The angel laughed. 'What are you doing, Fletcher? You realise you're only prolonging the inevitable?'

Was anything this guy said not a cliché?

I leapt again, this time into a customer getting his hair styled into little points that made him look like a crap dinosaur.

'Stop it,' demanded the angel.

Again and again, I leapt, moving from one body to another.

Find the lady.

The angel knotted his brow as he began to lose track of me. To make things even more challenging, I planted some suggestions in my hosts as I did the rounds, leaving each of them with an impression that they were dancing at a Christmas disco. Customers and hairdressers alike formed a line, each with his hands on the waist of the man in front.

'Choo choo choo!' they roared, shaking their hips, 'come on and do the conga!'

It's an imprecise science, the old out-of-body mind

control trick, only good for a few seconds after I've vacated a host, but good enough to allow for this caper.

The conga line snaked around the angel, forming a ring around him. Around and around the circle went, faster and faster, kicking their legs and belting out more *Black Lace* lyrics.

By this point the angel was completely lost; stupefied by the shell game I was playing. He spun about, trying to get an eye on me, muttering some distinctly non-kosher words under his holier-than-thou breath.

'Show yourself!' he screamed. 'I demand you show yourself!'

I would love to have seen the look on his face when he realised I'd hoofed it and taken Mark along for the ride too, but I suppose you can't have everything in this afterlife.

8
———

With that palaver out of the way, I returned to the job at hand.

It was around ten in the evening when I arrived at the Royal Free Hospital. The A&E's reception area smelled of bleach and a heady undertone of vomit. The walls were lit by harsh strip lighting and coated in scuffed magnolia paint scarred by the thousands of trolleys that had scraped by them over the years.

I checked behind the reception desk to see who'd been lumbered with night duty. I was in luck. A young woman sat plonked on a cheap bit of revolving furniture; not too pretty, not too smart looking. The perfect mark for my charm offensive.

'Hello love,' I chirped, as I swaggered over and placed my hands flat upon her desk. She looked up at me and I saw her eyes widen, just a smidge, but enough to let me know she was liking what she saw. 'I'm after a couple of your paramedics,' I told her. 'Two of your night shift boys.'

'Karl and Dimitrie?' she asked, taking her gum from her mouth and depositing it into a nearby bin.

'That's the ones,' I replied, making a mental note of their names. This was too easy.

'They're on call tonight,' she told me, fluttering her eyelashes. 'Is there anything I can help you with?'

'There is as a matter of fact. See, they were round my mum's gaff a few hours back. Came by after she took a spill—'

'Oh no, is she okay?'

'She is now, thank God,' I replied, allowing Mark's eyes to mist up, then looking away. 'The old bird's getting on in years and… well, I don't know what I'd do without me mum…'

I stole a glance at the receptionist as I choked back a hot sob. She made an *"Awww"* face and placed a warm hand on top of mine. I smiled. I was worried the old *loving son* act might come over a bit Norman Bates, but from the looks of things, it was working a treat.

I cleared my throat. 'Anyway, Mum tried my phone first but I wasn't able to pick up.'

'Why not?'

'I'm embarrassed to say it, but I was driving a busload of special needs kids at the time, and I didn't have my hands-free.'

The receptionist melted some more. 'You help special needs kids for a living?'

'Oh no,' I said, 'just in my spare time.'

By this point she was putty in my hands.

'After I didn't pick up, Mum rang 999,' I went on, 'and from what she tells me, your ambulance blokes were with her in five minutes flat.'

'That's great.'

'Too right it is… sorry, what was your name…?'

'Tracey,' she replied, unflinchingly.

'Tracey,' I said, smiling. 'That's a nice name. So, like I was saying, Karl and Dimitrie got to her like a bullet out of a gun, and according to Mum, they were amazing. Really went above and beyond. Got her back on her feet, fixed her a cuppa, even stuck around to play a game of Hearts with her during their tea break.'

'That's nice.'

'Too right. And mum's not usually great with strangers either, especially ones that ain't from around here if you know what I mean.'

She chuckled. 'Yeah, my mum's a bit like that as well.'

We shared a laugh, then I moved on to phase two of my plan. 'Thing is, while they were at Mum's, one of them managed to leave this behind...' I held up a wallet. It was Mark's wallet, but she didn't need to know that.

'That's good of you to bring that in,' she said. 'Not many good samaritans left in this world.'

She reached for the wallet but I snatched it back.

'Thing is, I'd like to return it myself. Personally, like.'

She seemed surprised. 'It's no trouble.'

'Don't get me wrong, Tracey, it's not that I'm not grateful, it's just...' I whispered, leaning across her desk conspiratorially; a move she was only too happy to mirror... 'I thought maybe if you gave me an address I could drop it off myself, along with a little something to say thank you.'

'Hm, whose wallet is it, Karl or Dimitrie's?' she asked, then decided it wasn't important. 'Actually, it doesn't matter, they both live in the same place.'

'Well, that makes life easier, doesn't it?' I joked. Seemed Jazz had been right; the vamps were cohabiting.

I pulled a piece of paper from my pocket and slid it across the reception desk. 'Do us a favour, Tracey, scribble that address down for me, would you?' I gave her a wink.

'And maybe bung your phone number on there while you're at it...'

She giggled and reached for a pen, but then— 'What am I thinking?' she said. 'I can't give that out, it's data protected.'

Ugh, so close.

'Come on, Tracey,' I said, giving her the old puppy dog eyes, 'let's not get all wrapped up in the rules...'

'I'm sorry,' she replied, 'it's more than my job's worth. Why don't you just give it to me to pass on? I promise I'll take good care of it.'

Damn it. So much for my charm offensive.

Plan B it was then.

I don't like to play the possession card, I really don't, but she was leaving me no choice. Forcing your will on someone is a creepy thing to do, but forcing your will on a woman... that's something I like to stay clear of altogether unless it becomes absolutely necessary. Thing is, stopping a couple of Draculas from draining another poor sod dry fit that criteria like a glove.

I left Mark with a message to stay put then pulled the ripcord, passing from his body, through the reception desk, and into Tracey. She wasn't a tough nut to crack. Within a few seconds, I'd taken control of her brain and rifled through her mental Rolodex to find the information I needed. She didn't have the address I was after committed to memory, but she did have the location of the staff records and the password to get at them.

I rolled her chair over to her workstation, accessed the database and tapped in the necessary digits. A quick search of Dimitrie brought up his record, only instead of finding contact info, all I found were a few lines of asterisks. No address, no phone number, not even an email. Same for

Karl. They'd covered their tracks well. Shit. This trip had been a total waste of time.

Annoyed, I implanted a bit of conversational filler in Tracey's head to cover the last couple of minutes I'd spent digging around in her brain, then jumped back into my ride.

'Thanks anyway,' I told her, replacing Mark's wallet in his pocket before making off.

'Wait,' she called after me, 'your bit of paper...'

'Keep it,' I said.

'But I didn't give you my number...'

As I exited the building, the hospital doors sighed shut behind me, making a sound like I felt. What the hell was I going to do now? Any minute now Mark's body was going to reject me, and I wouldn't be able to go back to him after that for fear of being rumbled by the angel again. I was proper fucked now. Being intangible made being a detective nigh on impossible... or should I say *"playing"* a detective. I mean, it's not like I have a P.I. licence or anything. I make this job up as I go along really. I take my cues from TV shows and film noirs, old pulp novels and Humphrey Bogart movies. I'm just a dead man with a thing for gumshoes, that's all. The fact is, I knew as much about being a P.I. as I did about being an exorcist.

Yeah, I was having myself a real pity party. I strode through the hospital car park, looking for something to kick or a car aerial to snap, except of course cars don't come with those anymore.

Then I saw it.

There, sat in a staff parking bay... a long, black hearse. A 1960 Superior Cadillac Hearse, to be precise, with polished chrome stylings and a giant speaker system where a coffin would sit. Hanging from the rearview mirror was a plush toy of Count Dracula. I shook my head in disbelief.

'You're having a laugh...' I actually said out loud.

I may have been a bit generous when I attributed two brain cells to this pair of clowns.

I pressed my face up against the driver's window and took a peek inside the car. Stuck to the windscreen, just above the dash, was a sat nav unit. Perfect. Having checked to make sure the coast was clear, I pressed my hand against the driver's door and used a simple bit of magic to jimmy it open.

Did I mention that I was a magician? I meant to say something about it up top, but I worried the info dump was stacking up high enough already without me adding more to the pile. You know, what with all the ghost stuff and everything. I didn't want to come on too strong, so I decided to portion the story out. One thing at a time, I told myself.

So yeah, I know a bit of magic. I used to dabble back when I was an exorcist, but I decided to dedicate myself to it properly after I carked it. It's still very much a work in progress. Right now the best I can manage are a few simple cantrips: a glowing light here, a magic flame there, that sort of stuff. None of your Gandalf the Grey shit. If it's real magic you're after, talk to Jazz Hands, or better yet, my witch's familiar friend, Stella. That girl can sling a spell eight ways to Sunday.

If I do have a knack for one thing, though, it's unlocking stuff. Show me a bolt, a latch or a padlock and I'll have it open in a jiffy. I've had safes open before. Big ones. Compared to that, popping a car door was a piece of piss.

I reached inside the vehicle and laid my hands on the sat nav. I turned it on and checked the device's GPS settings. There it was, a few notches below the last inputted location; an address.

An address marked *Home*.

9

Seeing as I couldn't drop Mark off at his pad in case the angel was sat there waiting for me, I left him in a nearby boozer with a few empty pint pots and a half-done crossword (just the easy answers filled in, obviously).

With that business out of the way, I went to the address I'd lifted from the hearse's TomTom and staked the place out.

Castle Dracula it was not.

The vampire den turned out to be a semi-detached house on a nice, leafy street; well looked-after once, but gone to the dogs now. Its empty driveway was strewn with uncollected rubbish: crisp packets, cigarette butts and old, sun-bleached Coke cans. The front garden had been left to grow wild, and the manicured ivy that climbed the front of the house now crept over the window panes and into the gutters.

I pulled out my mobile, scrolled through my contacts and gave Stella a bell. I promised Jazz Hands I wouldn't tackle these guys solo, and I intended to keep my word.

The phone rang, and rang, then went to voicemail. 'Stella, it's Jake Fletcher, the Ghost with the Most. I've got a situation going on with some vampires. Call me when you get this, it's urgent.'

I stayed where I was, stood across the road from the house, casing the joint. Hours passed. It was getting on for five in the morning when I heard a car engine and looked up to see a hearse pull up around the corner and park in the driveway.

As I watched from the shadows, two men stepped out of the vehicle and headed inside the property. I checked my watch. The sun would be up soon and they'd be sound asleep in their coffins. There'd be no better time to strike.

I tried Stella's number again. Still no answer. Shit. If I didn't do something soon I was going to miss my window. I couldn't let that happen. I said I wouldn't go in there alone, but what else was I supposed to do? Lives were at stake, and I sure as hell wasn't putting DCI Stronge at risk by dragging her into a vampire den.

I patted the grenades in my pockets. 'Sorry, Jazzer. A job's a job.'

I cracked my knuckles and crossed the road to the house.

As I passed through the rusty front gate and crept up the house's cracked concrete path I checked the windows to make sure I wasn't being spied on through the gaps in the ivy. Unlike regular folks, vampires can see ghosts, so I had to be extra careful. This wouldn't be a welcome house call.

I walked up the steps of the front porch and entered the house without breaking my stride. No need for magic this time. Instead, I phased through the front door and arrived directly in the house's hallway, no tarting about.

The place was as much an eyesore on the inside as it was the out. The polished teakwood floor had turned dull from neglect, and a thick layer of dust lay on every surface. The place was a mess. As I passed along the hallway I took a peek in a room off to one side. It was a baby's bedroom, with a colourful mural of a monkey on the far wall and a crib in its centre. Just like the rest of the house, this too was blanketed in dust.

I felt a knot in my stomach.

Returning to the hallway I saw a framed picture, face down on a sideboard. I made my hand corporeal and carefully stood it up. It was a family photo, a studio portrait of a single mother, and sat on her shoulders, a little girl of maybe six months old. My jaw tightened. The vampires had done something terrible here. A mother and her child, drained dry, their bodies done away with, their happy home turned into a tomb. Judging by the state of the front garden the intruders had been squatting here for months too, which meant no one had come calling. The vamps had done their homework. All this mother and daughter had was each other, and those bloodsucking bastards had snacked on them like two fingers of a Kit Kat. I lay down the picture and took out one of my grenades. Those fuckers were going to pay for that.

At the end of the hallway, I found a wooden door under the house's main staircase. Beyond the door was a flight of steps that dipped into the thick darkness of the cellar like a quill into an inkwell. I crept down the steps slowly, not because I was worried about upsetting a creaky floorboard —I don't weigh anything—but to savour the moment. I smiled, relishing the prospect of turning those parasites into a pair of smoking ash piles.

The cellar was low-ceilinged, dank, and covered in

mould. Its tiny, street-level windows had been painted black and covered with pieces of cardboard. The only light came from the faint glow of the hallway upstairs, which outlined various piles of junk: overstuffed bin liners, battered boxes, and cobwebbed exercise equipment.

I expected to find some coffins down there in the gloom, maybe a sarcophagus or two, but instead I found a couple of piles of rags with a waxy body lying on each, arms folded across their chests. It was a healthy reminder that real vampires weren't the romantic creatures from a Bram Stoker novel, or sultry teenagers glittering like ravers in a gay club. Real vampires are pink-eyed scumbags that leech off the living. Oversized vermin.

I felt the weight of the grenade in my hand and tossed it into the air a couple of times like a tennis player readying for a serve. Time to put those bastards out of commission for good. I took a step forward and readied for my shot—

—when my phone rang.

Shit.

The vampires came up from their rag piles like coiled springs, hissing and spitting.

I raised the grenade over my head. 'Hold it there, Count Fuckulas,' I said. 'This thing's harmless to me, but it'll turn the two of you into little bitty ashes.'

They froze. They could see in my eyes that I wasn't mucking about.

Since they were awake now, I figured I might as well get some answers from them before I dropped the literal bomb. 'So go on then,' I said, 'why did you do it?'

The vampires looked to one another with their albino eyes. 'Do what?' replied the larger of the two.

'The street kid with the track marks and tattoo,' I said.

'You picked him up on your rounds a couple of nights back and dumped his body on the Heath. Why?'

They looked at each other again, then back to me.

'Dumped him on the Heath?'

'Cut the shit, I know full well it was you.'

The smaller one curled his lip. 'We only drank the blood. The husk was taken from us.'

I laughed. 'You expect me to believe that? What kind of a mug do you take me for?'

'It's the truth. We were about to dig a hole for the body out back when a visitor came.'

'Go on then,' I said, enjoying the yarn. 'Who was it? Father Christmas?'

The vampires both sneered this time. 'A man knocked at the door,' said the taller one. 'We did not know him, but he said he wanted to come inside.'

'And you just let him in?'

'He was... very persuasive.'

I found the idea of a suave, midnight caller a bit hard to swallow, but I played along anyway. 'So this mystery visitor of yours, what did he look like?'

'It is hard to say. He wore a hood.'

'What kind of a hood? A Klan hood?'

'No, the opposite kind,' he spat. 'The man was a negro.'

Charming. That's the way it is with vamps, though, they might look young, but most of them have been around since before slavery was abolished. Plus, being descended from a guy who planted babies on spikes doesn't exactly add to your chill.

'So let me get this right,' I said, kneading the bridge of my nose with my non-grenade hand, 'a black man in a hoodie shows up at your door asking to take a corpse away and you said *okey dokey*?'

'His words... he made us do as he asked,' replied the smaller one. 'Besides, he did us a favour taking the body. Saving us from having to dig another hole in the garden.'

'You want to know what I think?' I asked, certain they didn't. 'I think you made this hooded bloke up. I think you dragged Fergal's body to the Heath, put a rock in his hand and made him bash in some bloke you were having a barney with.'

'You are wrong.'

'You know nothing, ghost,' said the other.

It seemed they were sticking to their story. Fine. Their testimony was obviously bullshit, which made them the guilty parties. Soon as I'd dealt with them, Fergal got his wings and this case was closed.

'Well, it's been nice talking to you gents,' I said, giving the grenade one last squeeze, 'but I reckon I'm going to call it a day.'

Time to light the place up. I pulled the pin, wound up my throwing arm and tossed the UV bomb into the centre of the room—

But just as it landed, the smaller of the vampires snatched a tin bucket from a pile of junk, flipped it over, and slammed it down on the ground, muffling the explosion.

Poof.

The grenade detonated harmlessly under the light-proof container.

Bugger.

There was one frozen second, then I saw two sets of pink eyes flick my way.

'Easy there, lads,' I said, backing up.

The vampires pounced, fangs bared, saliva streaming down their waxy chins.

If you'll permit me to take a quick pause here, I'd like to spend a moment talking about fighting.

See, there are two kinds of brawls. First there's the movie kind: all Jackie Chan leg sweeps and bullet-time balletics. Then there's the real kind: scrappy, awkward, and done in a few seconds.

This was the second kind.

The real kind.

I didn't take my opponents down with a devastating double face kick.

I didn't make a nimble side-step and turn one's power against the other.

No.

I clocked the little vampire in the chin, and while he was flapping around on the floor, I kicked his mate square in the knackers.

Wallop. Wallop.

No pissing about.

Now, I know what you're thinking. *"Where did this guy learn to throw a punch?"* you ask. I get it. You see a bloke in a sharp suit and a tidy haircut and you think, *"if it comes to a ruckus, this one's going home with his head on backwards"*. It's cool, I can see your confusion. I know I don't look like I'd be much use in a scuffle, but believe me when I tell you I've learned to hold my own over the years. After that business with Mark and the handcuffs, I decided I'd had enough of getting kicked around. An all-boys Catholic school is no place for a victim, so instead of taking it on the chin the next time one of the big kids decided he wanted to boost his ego at my expense, I knocked some teeth down his throat.

I got tough.

Picked up some weights. Did some boxing. Tried out a martial art or two.

It didn't come easy. I took a lot of lumps on my way to being a half-decent scrapper. A lot of lumps. See, the thing about fighting is, you only really get good at it by doing a lot of it. Lucky for me, I was given plenty of opportunities to brush up on my skills. Day in, day out those kids came at me, and every time, I fought my corner. It didn't feel like I was being done any favours at the time, but here, outnumbered two-to-one and fighting on someone else's turf, I was grateful for every shove, every punch, every Chinese burn. Whatever happened to me next, it wouldn't happen quietly.

While the big vamp lay on the floor clutching his undead unmentionables, his pal staggered to his feet and came at me again. I put up my dukes and went to plant another fist in his face, but he was quick and managed to duck my swing.

He caught me with the butt of his shoulder and barged me to the ground.

Crash.

The pair of us went south in a messy heap, smashing through a stool piled high with old magazines and sending splintered wood and yellowed pages every which way. As we hit the concrete floor, I tried to roll with the fall so I ended up on top of my attacker, but he was having none of it. Instead, he kept the high ground and started raining down blows on my face. I got my arms up to defend myself, though, which forced him to find a new spot to inflict pain on.

Shifting his weight, he dug his knee into my chest and pressed down hard. He did it with such force and with such conviction that I felt the bones of my ribcage buckle and spread. Being a ghost, pain isn't something I get to feel every day. Physically speaking, most things pass right through me, whether I want them to or not. For that reason, it's easy to lose touch with the simple sensation of... well, touch. Blinding agony? That's something I hadn't felt for a good, long while. Don't get me wrong, it's not that I enjoy the act of getting hurt, but sometimes it's nice to be reminded that I am at least semi-alive. Not that I was about to thank the bloodsucker crushing my ribcage for it.

I elbowed the vampire in the jaw but it only served to piss him off. Snarling, he went to put my eyes out with his claws, but I managed to get my hands around his wrists just in time. He was unnaturally strong, though, and despite my best efforts, the pointed tips of his thumbnails edged closer and closer to my eyeballs. As he bore down on me with all his might, I turned my head to avoid a blinding.

That's when I saw it.

A broken stool leg, snapped from its seat during our fall.

The vamp saw what I was looking at and pressed down even harder.

He managed to get his hands to my face and hooked his thumbs into my eye sockets.

I felt the tip of his claws graze my eyelids.

Felt them scrape against the fragile membranes.

I saw the wooden leg. Saw its sharp, splintered end.

I'd only get one chance at this.

One chance to snatch it up and plug it in this fucker's back.

But turning a hand solid enough to do that required concentration.

The kind of concentration the vampire wasn't leaving much room for.

'Die!' he hissed.

It was now or never.

I let go of his wrist and shot a hand out for the chair leg.

Felt my fingers wrap around it.

And with everything I had, I rammed it home.

The sharp end entered his back right between the shoulder blades and sank in deep.

The vampire's eyes shot open wide. 'Wha—?' he gurgled and coughed up a glob of rich, red blood.

I whacked the chair leg with the heel of my palm, driving it home so hard it almost shot through the vamp's chest.

'Have some of that!' I roared, as he gasped and went slack on top of me.

Jazz Hands was right.

No one likes a stake through the heart.

I rolled the bloodsucker off and clambered to my feet just in time to see his mate, Billy Big Bollocks, untwist his nutsack and come at me for round two.

I'd had enough of the rough stuff for one day, so I went for the second grenade and pulled the pin.

I shielded my eyes, expecting the cellar to be flooded with brilliant, cleansing light. Instead, the grenade fizzled like a soggy firework, and with one final sputter, died.

'Oh, shit,' I said.

'You're going down,' said the vamp with a razor blade smile, and he darted towards me, teeth gnashing.

Panicking, I did the only thing I could think to do with the dud grenade and hurled it at the nearest blacked-out window. Thankfully, my aim was true, and the lump sailed over the vamp's shoulder and tore through the glass.

A knife of sunlight struck him in the back and sent him sprawling, and I used the moment of opportunity to slam my heel down on his skull. As he lay there floundering, I grabbed him by the neck and rammed him against the nearest wall.

'Tell me the truth!' I demanded.

'What truth?'

'About the body!' I screamed. 'Why did you do that with Fergal's body?'

With both hands on the vampire's throat, I forced him towards the lozenge of sunshine that had settled on the brick wall. As I inched the vamp's head into the light, strands of his hair caught fire, burning to their roots like lit fuses. He fought and hissed and spat, but I clung on to him, refusing to let go.

'Do you want to die?' I hollered.

'No!'

'Then admit it! Admit that you fitted Fergal up!'

Smoke poured from the bloodsucker as I pushed him fully into the light. I was grilling him in every sense of the word. The flesh on his forehead began to pucker and crisp, sizzling like cooked bacon.

'We had nothing to do with that!' the vamp screamed, then, with one last, desperate, pain-fuelled burst of adrenalin, fetched me a blow to the skull that dropped me like a bag of hammers.

Crack.

My head was spinning.

I shook off the tweeting birdies and looked up to see the vampire looming over me.

'Did you really think you could beat me, ghost?' he asked, ejecting a set of needle-sharp claws.

'Beat you?' I replied. 'Mate, I'm going to bury you so deep Google won't be able to find you.'

He chuckled. 'That's good. You're a funny man, you know that?'

'Oh yeah,' I replied. 'One way or another I'll have you in stitches...'

I sprung up and slugged the vamp in the face. He

recoiled, stunned, and I followed up with a barrage of blows, punching, kicking, kneeing, putting some real divots in the guy. I wouldn't take him down—a bloke his size could take whatever I threw at him—but the plan was never to deck him. The plan was to get him to the other side of the room. To get him to the window covered by that flimsy piece of cardboard...

Darting out a hand, I snatched a corner of gaffer tape and whipped off the makeshift blind. Sunlight streamed through the window, providing a firewall between the two of us that the vampire couldn't cross. Matter of fact, he couldn't even get out from his corner. I had him boxed in good and proper.

'Ready to talk now?' I asked.

The vampire crouched into a panting ball.

'It won't do you any good staying schtum, mate,' I told him. 'The sun's coming up still, and at the rate it's moving your way, you're gonna be toast in about five minutes flat.'

He shuffled backwards, drawing tight into his corner, the sunlight nibbling at his bare toes. 'Go to Hell,' he hissed.

'Reckon that's more your department,' I replied, watching as he drew back his feet and pulled his knees into his chest. 'Of course, I could always put that bit of cardboard back and we could call this a day. I mean, just so long as you tell me what Fergal's body was doing out there on the Heath.'

'How many times do you need to hear it?' he screeched. 'A man came. A man in a hood. He took away the body and that's all I know!'

I narrowed my eyes at him. Even under duress, the vamp was sticking to his story. For all the implausibility of it, it was starting to sound annoyingly like the truth.

The wall of sunlight had him completely hemmed in

now. He stood, sucking in his stomach to avoid its fiery wrath. 'Well?' he cried. 'You said you were going to help me!'

I remembered the picture on the sideboard upstairs. The one of the mother and daughter. I remembered the crib collecting dust.

'I lied,' I said, and turned my head just as the screaming started.

10

Dealing with those bloodsuckers had left a real knot in my head, and my body felt like it had been bounced down a flight of stairs built by M.C. Escher.

I ransacked the rest of the vampire den before I left. In the back garden, I uncovered a fresh grave plot, and around that, several more disturbed patches of earth where other bodies had been buried. To the back of the garden I saw thriving flowers, fertilised no doubt by the husks of even older victims, long since turned to compost. Given time, I'd do everything in my power to make sure those victims were tracked down and shown the way to the Good Place, but until then I had a promise to keep.

A quick visit to the roadside Fergal was haunting told me that he'd yet to be released from the material plane. Executing the vampires would only have brought Fergal justice so long as they were the last pieces of the puzzle, and since the midnight caller story seemed to have some ring of truth to it, Fergal wasn't permitted to depart this plane. Not yet, anyway. Not until I'd figured out how he'd really wound up on the Heath and made the perpetrator pay for it. Until then he was stuck here, trapped between this world and the next, degenerating day by day. I had to work fast. It wouldn't be long before Fergal became a wailing phantom, no more human than a bitter wind.

No. I wasn't about to let that happen.

If what the flash-fried vampire had told me was true—and I had every reason to believe that it was—I needed to uncover the identity of this midnight caller and make him answer for what he'd done. Whatever that was. I still had no clue why he'd set Fergal up as the murderer of some random skinhead.

So, what to do now? My first thought was to go back to my office and take stock of the situation, except chances were the avenging angel would be cooling his heels there waiting for me to drop by. If he'd done his homework he'd know all of my favourite haunts, which meant no more visits to Frosty and no more drop-ins on Jazz Hands. The last one was particularly annoying as I really wanted to have a chat with her about that dud grenade she'd palmed me off with. For someone so concerned for my safety, she had a bloody funny way of showing it.

Keeping clear of that do-gooder angel meant staying on the move and avoiding my usual hangouts, but that didn't mean my whole support structure was out of bounds. To solve this case I'd need information, equipment, muscle maybe. They wouldn't come easy now, but just because I was being hunted, didn't mean I couldn't call upon help every once in a while. After all, I wouldn't save Fergal alone. Pulling this off was going to require a team effort.

'Here,' whispered DCI Stronge, sliding a manilla envelope across the table.

We were sat in a booth at a backstreet dive bar called The Black Heart. *The Heart*, as it was more commonly known to its patrons, was my kind of hole: a *none more black* boozer that played Sabbath and Maiden loud enough to make your teeth rattle. The place appealed to a select crowd, and its corners were dank to the point of being stygian, making it the perfect spot for a private conversation. I'd chosen The Heart as our rendezvous spot for this reason, and because I'd only been there once before, a long time ago, back when I was still drawing breath.

'Could you open it up for me?' I said, looking down at the envelope.

'Oh right, yeah,' replied Stronge.

Being mostly intangible, fine motor skills aren't exactly my strong suit; something Stronge had a habit of forgetting. It was understandable. To someone with The Sight, I looked about as solid as anyone else in the establishment. To anyone else, Stronge was just a woman sat on her own muttering to herself, a not uncommon sight in Camden.

She checked we weren't being watched and spread the contents of the envelope out in front of me. I peered at the documents, inspecting them under the dim light of an upside-down neon crucifix. Among them were copies of identity records, mug shots, and a rap sheet thicker than a preacher's bible. They pertained to the second dead body discovered on the Heath. The skinhead.

'His name's Viktor Abdulov,' said Stronge. 'A.K.A. Valery Popov, A.K.A. Mikhail Sokolov. It wasn't easy coming by an ID; it took Interpol to provide the match.'

'You've been busy,' I replied. I scanned Viktor's list of known associates. 'Says here he's mobbed up.'

'*Was* mobbed up,' Stronge corrected. 'He cut ties with the Bratva when he fled Moscow and came here.'

'Any idea why he jumped ship?'

'Nothing on record.'

'What else do we know about the guy?' I asked, pointing at one of Viktor's eight-by-ten glossies.

'Only that he was ripe for a clobbering,' replied Stronge. 'According to the Russian authorities he did jail time back home; multiple stretches for GBH and murder. There's some kidnapping and sexual assault in there too. No one's going to mourn this guy.'

That certainly fit my theory as to why his ghost was absent from the crime scene. Any one of those items on his rap sheet would put his soul on a slippy slide to Hell.

'Well?' I said. 'Aren't you going to ask me what I've been up to?'

Stronge sighed. 'Go on then, what have you been up to?'

'Funny you should ask. I just single-handedly beat the crap out of two vampires. Don't like to brag about it, though.'

I told Stronge about my quest to find Fergal's ghost, and how it had led me to the bloodsuckers and their tale of a door-knocking corpse collector.

'Jesus,' she blurted, raking a hand through her bob. 'So what now? Where do we go from here?'

'I don't know,' I said, 'but when I've figured it out I'll let you know.'

I was about to say my goodbyes when a bloke the size of Meatloaf squeezed into my side of the booth and right into my lap. Like, literally into my lap. Being ethereal and half his size, he managed to take up the space I was occupying and more besides, blotting me out completely.

'Can I get you a snakebite, darling?' he slurred at Stronge, totally oblivious to my presence.

Some people really have no manners.

11

Having watched DCI Stronge rebuff Meatloaf's unwelcome advances (the aftermath of which makes me cross my legs just thinking about it) I headed out to decide what I was going to do next. My meeting with Stronge had ended up posing more problems than solutions. I needed answers, but I wasn't going to find them on Stronge's side of the law. To get the real nitty-gritty I'd need to take a walk on the wild side. To kick in some doors and shake down some scumbags. And if ever there was a scumbag in this town, it was Camden's own kingpin of crime, Vic Lords.

Vic knew the borough's seedy underbelly like no one else. If there was something rotten going on in these parts he almost certainly had a hand in it, and if he didn't, he'd know the man who did. No one got up to mischief in Vic's manor without his say so. He was Mr Big. Numero Uno. Top of the arsehole pyramid.

It cuts me up to this day that I used to work for the guy. What can I say? I was young, I needed the money. London isn't exactly flush with exorcist jobs, but somehow Vic had the hook-up to every gig going. East to West and both sides of the River, if there was a haunting in this city, that man knew about it. All of this to make some coin of course. His system was to buy up spooked properties at rock bottom rates, send me in to cleanse them, then flog them on for a tidy profit. Meanwhile, I got a regular paycheque for doing the one thing in this world that I was actually good at. Everyone was a winner.

Well, not everyone.

As it turns out, gaming the housing market was just one of Vic Lords' corrupt little schemes. I later learned that his interests included illegal gambling, drug dealing, sex trafficking, and more besides. Like a modern-day Hitler, he also grew to develop a hard-on for all things occult, and took to spicing up his nefarious deeds with a dash or two of the old diabolism. The damage Vic Lords has done to this city is incalculable, but somehow he always stays the right side of a jail cell. He's smart, well organised, and has enough layers of insulation between him and his underlings to ensure that the law can never connect him to his criminal activities. The police can't touch him.

But that didn't mean I couldn't.

I pictured Lords' place of business, a squalid little office above a knocking shop near the canal, and readied to make the jump there. I was just about to do my thing when something completely unexpected happened. A battered grey limousine with blacked-out windows pulled up alongside me, screeched to a halt and ejected two brawny men in cheap suits. The goons came at me with intention, seized me by the wrists and shoved me into the rear seat of the vehicle. It happened so fast that it took me by complete surprise, and the next thing I knew I was sandwiched between the two heavies and facing their boss.

'Hello, Jake,' said the odious man sat opposite as the limo sped off with me inside. 'It's been a while.'

Speak of the devil.

Vic Lords took a drag on the stub of his cigar. 'How you been keeping?' he asked.

'Oh, you know,' I replied, 'still dead.'

Vic smiled that smile of his; the one that even managed to give a ghost the creeps. He leaned forward in his seat so I could get a better look at him. His bouffant of unnaturally dark hair had been slicked back with Brylcreem, and his pale, sweaty skin was criss-crossed with a web of collapsed blood vessels, making him look as though he'd been cut from a wheel of rotten Stilton.

'Thanks for joining me,' he said, exhaling a thick lance of smoke that left the gloomy interior of the limo looking like a hot-boxed ride on its way to Glasto.

'Thanks for saving me a trip,' I replied. 'I was about to pay you a visit, Vic.'

One of the goons tightened his grip on my arm and sneered. 'That's "Mister Lords" to you,' he barked.

His teeth were small and sharp, like a piranha's. He wasn't human, he was an eaves, an Uncanny creature that was capable of harming ghosts. Lords must have hired him and his friend with that in mind. Of course, whether his men could touch me or not, there was nothing they could do to stop me ghost-bouncing away and giving them the slip altogether.

'So what's your game, Vic?' I asked. 'You finally planning on doing away with me?'

He laughed. 'And why would I do that? I've got a soft spot for you, Fletcher, always have. You were one of my best employees once, don't forget that.'

The chance would be a fine thing. Choosing to work

with Lords was one of the most regrettable decisions of my life. I'd say a good 90% of the red in my ledger came down to my association with that scumbag.

'Well, so long as we're best friends,' I said, 'why don't you tell me what you know about the two dead bodies on the Heath?'

'Only too happy to help, Jake. Why else do you think I went to all this trouble?'

I offered him a thin smile. 'Let's hear it then. What do you know?'

'That's not very polite,' he replied, full of mock displeasure. 'I'm offering you a present, Jake. And what do we say to people who give us presents?'

It caught in my throat but I forced myself to say it. 'Thank you.'

He grinned so wide I thought the corners of his mouth might leave his face and meet at the back of his head. 'You're welcome,' he said, and leaned in even closer. 'The present is this: a warning. The man you're chasing is best left alone. You're out of your element with this one, Fletcher, take it from me.'

'Where are you getting this?'

'Same place I get all my good ideas,' he replied, tapping his nose. 'A little birdie told me.'

That was Vic's code for augury. Since he started tapping into the dark arts he'd been using his powers to snoop on things outside of a normal man's purview. As far as I could tell, he used these divinations mainly for financial profit and to keep an edge on his competitors. In essence, to get behind the other players' backs and sneak a look at what cards they were holding. This was something different, though. Vic had seen something he didn't go looking for.

'The man in the hood is from another place,' he told me. 'A bad place.'

'He's some kind of demon?'

Pit fiends pushing their way in from The Nether were getting to be an all too common occurrence since the London Coven were wiped out. The protections that Stella Familiar's creators had put in place to keep demons and the like in check were gone now, leaving all hell to break loose in this city.

'Not a demon,' Vic replied. 'Something else. Something ancient. Something... legendary.'

'What are you telling me?'

'I'm telling you there's a new man in town, Jake, and he's not playing for either of our teams.'

'What am I supposed to do with that little titbit?' I asked. 'I've got a murder to solve, and nothing you've told me so far is going to help that happen.' I offered him a shrug. 'This so-called present you've given me is due a serious re-gifting.'

Vic sighed, disappointed. 'Don't do this to yourself, Jake. Leave it be. Let it go and don't look back.'

'Since when do you care what happens to me?'

'How many times do I have to say it? I like you. You've got some old-fashioned ideas about right and wrong, but we can work on that. Give up this P.I. lark and get back on the payroll. Make some real money for a change. We could be living the life, you and me.'

'I don't have a life, Vic. I'm dead.'

He grinned at me ghoulishly. 'You could always be deader.'

'Is that a threat?'

He blew out a long stream of smoke. 'Not from me it ain't.'

I'd gotten everything I was going to get from Camden's

kingpin of crime. 'Well, Vic,' I said, 'always a pleasure, but if you don't mind, I'm going to make a move.'

'Of course,' he replied. 'Off you toddle.'

I was about to bounce when he held up a finger and gave me the old, "One last thing".

'What is it?' I sighed.

'Just a bit of advice before you go.'

'Go on then, don't keep me in suspense.'

'Do yourself a favour, Jake. If you're not going to listen to me, at least watch your back out there. Mark my words, son, the four horsemen are saddling up, and they don't care who they trample.'

12

When I checked my phone I found three missed messages, all from DCI Stronge. I'd muted the thing after it almost got me killed in the vampire den, and hadn't noticed it buzzing in the back of Vic's limo.

I hit Return Call and Stronge picked up before the second ring.

'Where the hell have you been, Fletcher?' she barked.

Some might have mistaken her tone for anger, but I preferred to think of it as unresolved sexual tension.

'I was seeing a man about a dog,' I replied.

'One of these days I'm going to get a straight answer from you.'

'I wouldn't bet on it.'

She paused to take an exasperated breath. 'Well, while you were otherwise engaged, we caught another one.'

'Same MO?'

'Looks that way.'

It seemed the murder on the Heath had only been the beginning. 'Go on then,' I said, preparing myself for the worst. 'Lay it on me.'

'It happened just over an hour ago. A stabbing. Killer dropped dead at the scene, but his body was dead before it got there.'

'Wait... you're telling me the killer was dead but arrived on foot?'

'That's right.'

Corpses walking about of their own volition? It was starting to look like Stronge's zombie theory had some legs after all. Matter of fact, it was looking like she'd been spot on from the start. But who was behind all of this? Who was it making the dead kill?

'And you're saying all of this happened in broad daylight?' I asked. 'Surely there must have been witnesses?'

'Plenty, it happened at a kids' playground.'

'Jesus wept. Please tell me the victim was an adult.'

'Yeah,' she replied. 'But not the killer.'

That I didn't need to hear.

'Twelve-year-old boy,' Stronge went on. 'Strolled up to the vic with a kitchen knife and stabbed him in the back before collapsing.'

Whoever was behind this was one sick puppy. 'Where's the kid now?' I asked.

'Both bodies have been moved to the bone house.'

She meant the morgue. 'I'm not talking about the bodies. I'm talking about the ghosts.'

'No sign of either. Same as before.'

That added up. If this one really was a match for the murder on the Heath, the adult was on his way to the fiery pit already. The kid, though... the kid was out there somewhere, alone and scared out of his wits. 'I've gotta find him,' I said.

'Not without me, you won't.'

Stronge traced the juvenile's address to a nearby children's home, a care facility for local hard-luck cases. I knew places like this, I used to visit them as a kid when the Social would take me away after my mum's drunken rages. I'd never spend too long away from her, though, just enough time for her to complete an addiction programme, get the care order revoked, and then the cycle would start all over again. But this isn't about me. This is about a little boy called Mike Dunn who died and became a sicko's murder puppet.

Mike was just shy of thirteen years old and had lived at the children's home since his parents died in a car accident last winter, leaving him with no next of kin. It wasn't clear whether we'd find Mike's ghost at the home, but it was a good place to start. It was likely that whatever we encountered there would call for a certain degree of diplomacy, though, a quality DCI Stronge wasn't exactly noted for. While she is an expert at running down bad guys, Kat's matter-of-fact, no-beating-around-the-bush approach to police work had a habit of putting people's noses out. For that reason, it was begrudgingly agreed that Stronge be the face of this investigation, while I played her Cyrano.

The children's home was about as miserable a place as you'd imagine. A joyless, armpit of a building full of second-hand furniture and neglected people. A dumping ground for life's unwanted things. Stronge approached the reception area with me by her side, invisible to the naked eye. She flashed her warrant card and told the portly caregiver manning the front desk that she had some information about a child in her care.

Together, the three of us went to a stuffy, grey back

office, where Stronge gave the woman the bad news about Mike (leaving out the stuff about him laying his hands on a dagger and going all Mini Brute). Meanwhile, I worked alongside Stronge, cushioning her directness and injecting the proceedings with some much-needed tact. It was a heartbreaking conversation all the same, and the half box of balled up tissues it provoked left me with no doubt as to the caregiver's innocence.

'How long ago did you last see Mike?' Stronge asked, handing the woman another Kleenex on my instruction.

'Yesterday,' she sniffed. 'Around lunchtime.' She explained that she'd asked another of the boys after Mike's whereabouts that evening and been told he was staying with a friend. We learned later that the kid had been covering for Mike, and not for the first time, though the place he was vanishing to was a mystery.

I leaned across to Stronge. 'Ask her what she can tell you about Mike. What kind of a kid was he?'

Stronge parroted my words at her.

'He's—*he was*—a lovely little boy... especially given all the stuff he went through with his parents. Oh, God, it's so sad...'

Stronge just sat there like some cyborg.

'Show her some comfort,' I said. 'Put your arm around her. Tell her you're sorry. Something!'

Stronge huffed and leaned over to place a hand on hers, just for a second. 'There there,' she said, doing her best impression of a human.

The caregiver smiled weakly through her tears. Once she'd finished sobbing, I gave Stronge her next cue. 'Does she have any idea where he might have been going?'

She didn't. 'We're understaffed here and underfunded. The best we can do is give these kids a roof over their heads and a couple of square meals a day. We can't watch them twenty-four seven.'

'Had Mike been showing any signs of distress?' Stronge asked, unprompted.

'He was a quiet boy, but yes, he did seem to take a turn a few weeks ago. I asked him about it at the time but he said nothing was wrong.'

Stronge was about to reply, but I cut her off. 'Ask her if she knows what he was distressed about.'

Forgetting herself, Stronge turned and looked me right in the eye. 'Why don't you ask her your bloody self!' she snapped, fed up of being the go-between.

The caregiver looked at her like she'd lost her mind. 'Are you okay, Detective?'

'I'm sorry,' Stronge coughed, collecting herself. 'Um. Mike. Do you know why he might have been distressed?'

'I don't know,' the woman replied, still a little taken aback. 'They get up to things on the outside. Sometimes they mix with bad elements. It's hard to say.'

I was about to offer another prompt but the look on Stronge's face told me not to bother.

'Are there places he went that you do know about?' Stronge asked. 'A favourite hangout maybe?'

The caregiver thought on it. 'Some of the boys liked to play at a scrap yard nearby. They weren't supposed to, but they would anyway. That's the only place I can think of.'

She gave Stronge the address.

'I'll check it out,' I told Kat, and got a covert nod back from her.

'Thank you,' she told the caregiver. 'A couple of my officers will want to interview the rest of your children, but you've been very helpful today.' She put a comforting arm around her, finally. 'We're very sorry for your loss.'

13

While DCI Stronge checked out the address of the stab victim, I followed up at the scrap yard.

The lead took me to a patch of abandoned wasteland tucked behind the railway tracks running out of Chalk Farm Station. The area was enclosed by a high brick wall topped with barbed wire and broken glass. The chained side gate had fallen into disrepair, though, and featured a hole that was easily large enough for a boy of Mike's age to crawl through.

Inside, I found a locked porta cabin nestled among tottering piles of rusting cars. The bank had foreclosed on the yard years ago, so there was no one around to stop me giving the place a recce. I spent a few minutes exploring the area until, eventually, I found something out of place. It's a wonder I saw it among all the junk, but across the far side of the lot, I found a looped scrap of leather curled up on the ground. Half of a belt, child-sized. I looked above where it lay and saw something hanging from the bumper of one of the stacked cars. Buckled to it was the other end of the belt.

'Christ,' I muttered, looking from the noose to the gibbet.

A voice came from behind me. 'Who are you?'

I whirled around to see the ghost of a young boy. He wore a raw ligature mark around his neck and his face was streaked with tears. 'Mike?' I asked.

'How do you know my name?'

'It's okay,' I told him. 'I'm here to help.'

'He said the same thing,' Mike replied. 'The bad man. He said he wanted to help. Said he was my friend, but he was only pretending.'

'Who was he?'

The boy cast his eyes to the ground.

'That's okay,' I told him. 'You don't have to answer that. Would you tell me how you got here, though?'

He stayed staring at his shoes.

'My name's Jake,' I said. 'I work with the police. That's how I know your name.'

'If you're a policeman, where's your badge?'

'I don't have a badge. I'm not a policeman, I'm a private detective.'

'Like Sherlock?' he asked, suddenly excited. 'Like on the telly?'

'Yeah, kind of. Except I'm not played by Bumblebee Cabbagepatch.'

He snorted; he was warming to me.

'So how did you wind up in this place?' I asked. 'The bad man you mentioned, did he bring you here?'

'No!' he replied, forcefully. 'I... I came here to get away from him. For good.' His eyes flicked to the belt in my hand. Jesus, he'd done this to himself. What had happened to make him want to do that I wondered, but I knew enough altar boys growing up to hazard a guess.

'It's okay,' I told him. 'And listen, you're going to be all right, you hear me? No one can hurt you now.'

'That's because I'm dead, isn't it? Like you.'

It's hard enough explaining the facts of unlife to an adult, let alone to a kid of twelve years old, but I did what I had to do. 'You're going to be okay,' I told him. 'I'm on the case now.'

'The game is afoot,' the kid said, quoting his favourite TV show.

'Yeah,' I replied, popping the collar of my jacket theatrically. *'The game is afoot.'*

He smiled. 'And the man in the hood, is he your Watson?'

I felt my blood run cold. 'You saw a man in a hood?' Apparently, the vampires had been telling the truth about their mystery caller.

'He came here after I...' again, Mike looked to the scrap of belt.

'Was he a black man?'

'Yeah.'

'And he's the bad man you mentioned?'

'No, he's my friend!'

That definitely came out of nowhere. 'How do you mean?'

'He said he'd make the bad man go away. Forever.'

He explained how the man in the hood had visited him after he'd put his head in the noose. How he'd come by and talked with him, saying he was sorry for the things he'd been through and that he was going to make things right. 'After that, there was only one of me,' Mike added.

I was puzzled at first, until we talked some more and I realised that he was talking about his body. The man in the hood had taken his corpse, just like he had Fergal's, leaving only his ghost behind. 'So how did, um, the other one of you go?'

'All by himself,' he replied. 'The man in the hood put him on the ground, then he whispered something in his ear and off he went.' He mimed a soldier's march.

It seemed the Hooded Man was a necromancer. Someone with the power to re-animate the dead and make them march to the beat of his drum. Who was he, though? Who was this murderous puppet master, weaponising corpses? And what was his game? Why was he doing this? Had the mob contracted him to tie up some loose ends? Taken him on as their necromantic button man? And if they had, could I expect to see more walking corpses knocking people off on my patch? Both hits had been a success after all; what if this was just the start of something bigger?

I had to move quickly before the Hooded Man struck again, even if that meant leaving a little boy to fend for himself in an abandoned breaker's yard.

'Can you be brave for me, Mike?' I asked.

'Yeah,' he sighed, sensing what was coming.

I told him he had to stay here, at least for a little while. 'It won't be for long,' I said. 'I promise.'

'And after that?'

I forced a smile. 'After that, you can go see your mum and dad again.'

Stronge called to tell me to meet her at the stab victim's address. She said to bring a friend, which was code for, "Wear the meat suit."

'I'm not doing that Cyrano shit again,' she told me. 'Besides, I prefer your friend's face to your ugly mug.'

That hurt, I won't lie. Still, I did as she asked and commandeered Mark for the job. I felt kind of bad about getting so much use out of the guy, but what was he really missing out on other than banging gullible women and running up huge champagne bills with his douchebag banker chums?

I arrived at the address and presented my ID to the constables manning the front gate. A female P.C. took my driver's licence and checked it against an access list to make sure I had business being there. The list would classify that I was joining the team as a "psychic consultant". There was a reason for that. Before she gained The Sight, Stronge would summon me to a murder scene for the purpose of conferring with the victim's ghost and discovering who their killer was. Given the inevitable presence of other law officers, the "psychic" tag handily explained away my wild leaps of logic as clairvoyance, whilst simultaneously doing away with the need for any pesky "credentials". It didn't exactly make me the most popular kid in class, though.

The P.C. saw my name on the licence and rolled her eyes back so far it's a wonder she didn't get a look at her own brain. 'That way,' she said, thumbing the door.

I thanked her for her hospitality and stepped inside the house.

The smell was the first thing that hit me. The smell of animal faeces, black mould and sour milk. Then there was the state of the place. All that was left of the hallway was a thin crease of floor between two great walls of junk: cardboard boxes wrapped in parcel tape, tin cans half-filled with congealed paint, and seesawing piles of dusty old novels. Whoever the guy was that lived here, he was the Smaug of hoarding useless old shit.

I turned Mark's body sideways and shuffled along the

corridor to the lounge, where I found Stronge among a cluster of forensics officers. Surrounding them was yet more junk: Tupperware containers of old McDonald's Happy Meal toys, a giant, novelty whiskey bottle filled with loose change, a nativity set from who knows how many Christmases ago, and an arrangement of creepy porcelain dolls judging us silently from their seat on the sofa.

'It's going to take years to sort through this stuff,' Stronge muttered.

Something hairy scuttled by my leg and I yelped as I left the floor by an inch or two. When I looked up again I saw the eyes of the forensics officers boring into me over the tops of their breathing masks.

'I don't think they like me,' I whispered.

'Of course, they don't,' Stronge replied. 'They're men of science. You piss in the eye of that.'

Fair enough.

I changed the subject. 'So what are we thinking? I asked. 'We thinking this guy was mobbed up too?'

Stronge was mid-shrug when a female forensics officer appeared in the doorway. 'We've found something, Detective. You'd better come take a look.'

Following her, we picked our way up a flight of shoe-covered stairs to the landing, past a mountain of old machine parts and into a bedroom that was in even more need of downsizing than the rest of the house. It looked like a jumble sale that had fallen victim to a hurricane.

'There,' said the officer, pointing to a computer sitting on a desk piled high with old drink cans and plates used as makeshift ashtrays. The machine was switched on, and displayed on the screen above its cigarette-scarred keyboard, an indecent image of a child. 'There's a trove of it on there,' she added, sickened.

I turned away from the screen. I couldn't look at it.

Kat had a stronger stomach. 'Well,' she said. 'I guess that explains what the vic was doing hanging around at a kiddie's playground.' She snapped on a pair of latex gloves and went snooping through the computer's hard drive. After a couple of minutes of investigation, she tapped the screen and turned to me. 'Yep, it's what I thought.'

She showed me a file marked "Cherub Club."

'A colleague working for the Child Protection Unit told me about this,' she said. 'He's spent the last six months chasing this dirty mac brigade as part of a special crime squad called Operation Paladin. The club had a dozen members at least, trading pictures of minors like hard cash. His squad rounded them up and booked them with conspiracy to distribute. All but one anyway.'

The man in the hood had dealt out a little vigilante justice it seemed. But why bring little Mike into this?

'Jesus,' said Stronge, pulling away from the computer.

She'd found another image. An image of Mike, unclothed, posed like no child should ever be posed. The background of the photo was a match for the lounge, complete with creepy porcelain dolls.

'Turn it off,' I said.

I hated this case. Hated it. This isn't what I became a P.I. for. I got into this game for the Sam Spade stuff. Stalking the mean streets, swigging scotch from the bottom drawer, late-night calls from double-crossing dames with long gams. Not... this. Not porn rings and child molesters and dead kids. I'd take real demons over this any time. That's the kind of evil I want to be dealing with. The old-fashioned, biblical kind. An evil that parades around with horns on its head, stinking of brimstone, belching fire. Human monsters are so much worse.

Human monsters don't wear horns, they hide beneath the surface, silent and unseen, like snakes slithering under leaves.

'Turn it off!' I shouted.

Finally, Stronge pulled the plug.

I bet Stella Familiar never had to go through stuff like this. Trawling through a paedo's sex dungeon and looking at pictures of naked children. No, I bet she was out there tossing fireballs at some interdimensional ne'er-do-well, having the time of her life.

I put Stella out of my mind and returned to the job at hand. 'They were connected,' I said. 'Mike and this piece of shit knew each other.'

This had nothing to do with a mob hit. The kid and the paedophile had a past that didn't involve gangsters at all. So, the whole mobster angle, was it just a red herring? Had the ex-Bratva on the Heath had his skull caved in for reasons other than his former gang affiliations? Was he connected to Fergal somehow, the overdosed runaway? Connected in a personal way? It didn't seem possible, and yet I couldn't rule it out until I'd done some digging.

I went back to Fergal with a photo in my hand.

'Do you recognise this man?' I asked, pulling him into a side street and showing him the Russian's picture.

He gulped. 'Aya. Aye, I do.'

'How?'

'It was just after I arrived in London.' He took a breath. 'I was out one night. At a bar on Old Compton Street. There was this toilet stall with a hole in it and... well, you know...?

Yeah, I knew, and it had nothing to do with playing the piccolo.

I'd suspected Fergal might be gay. The witness I spoke to in the underground shanty town told me he'd never tried anything on with her, and I had a feeling there was more to that than him just being a gentleman. 'Carry on,' I said.

'Okay. Well, I put it through the hole and he grabbed it. Hard. Too hard. Then he started... cutting.'

Christ. 'He had a knife?'

'Aye. I managed to get away, though... but not before he... did some damage.'

I remembered Fergal's mutilated body on the mortuary slab and winced.

'I wasnae able to go after him,' he said, 'but I got a look at his face as he was legging it.' He stabbed the photo with his index finger. 'That's him.' Tears sprang up in Fergal's eyes. 'It all went wrong after that. I got on the scag, I lost my flat...' he trailed off.

So I was right. Fergal and the Russian were connected after all, and not in a friendly way. And just like little Mike, Fergal had been given a chance at revenge from beyond the grave. His mutilator had been out on Hampstead Heath that night, up to his old tricks no doubt, and got more than he bargained for. The mobster angle had been a red herring after all. The connection between Fergal and the Russian had nothing to do with gang crime; it was a hate crime that joined their fates.

A kiddie-fiddler stabbed in the back by a child he'd taken advantage of, and a gay-basher brained to death by a former victim. The corpses of the brutalised, re-animated and used to exact revenge. The Hooded Man was dishing out something more than justice. This was *ironic* justice. This was killing by design.

14

I told DCI Stronge to get some shuteye while I carried on the investigation overnight. She protested, telling me she could power through, but she was dog tired and we both knew it. As for me, I had to do something to keep my mind occupied, and even if I were able to sleep I couldn't have. This case had gotten into my head, and I wouldn't let up until the Hooded Man had answered for what he'd done.

Before I said goodnight to Stronge, she mentioned that Dr Anand was carrying out the autopsies of Mike and his abuser that evening, so I decided to ditch the meat suit and pay a visit to the morgue for an observe and report. Don't get me wrong, I didn't relish the prospect of watching Anand carve a giant Y into a dead kid, but if there was any chance of her examination leading me to the man in the hood, I was going to be there.

As I'd been informed, Dr Anand was there, dressed in her scrubs and apron, burning the midnight oil. As she worked, I stood by inconspicuously in my ghost form, watching her unseen. Anand began with a cursory examination of the adult, the cadaver of which lay on its fat belly, presenting a back full of holes. She inspected the corpse visually and reported her findings into a microphone that hung above the autopsy slab.

'...Multiple sharp force injuries from a rear, dropped position consistent with the witness report of a juvenile stabber. I count... eleven puncture wounds and... five chops. Cause of death at this stage seems self-explanatory.'

She moved across to the opposite slab and began to examine the body of Mike, which lay on its back, facing the ceiling. He looked peaceful. Except for the belt mark around his neck, he might as well have been sleeping.

'Come on,' I whispered, goading Anand on inaudibly. 'Give me something. Find me a clue. Lead me to the puppet master.'

Anand went about her second exam with the same dispassionate professionalism as the first. 'Without opening the body up and studying its internal organs, it would appear this death occurred due to strangulation.' She picked one of the cadaver's legs up by the heel and flexed it at the knee. 'Going by the degree of rigor mortis, the time of death is estimated to have occurred at least twelve hours ago.' She put the limb down and pinched the bridge of her nose in frustration. 'Which of course is impossible as the deceased was seen to perform a frenzied homicide less than four hours ago by at least a dozen witnesses.'

That part was no news to me, even if the re-animator's motive, method and identity were an utter enigma.

Anand went on. 'Continuing my examination, I will now conduct an internal exploration of the cadaver.'

She went to a tray of stainless steel instruments and selected a large scalpel. This was the part I'd been dreading.

I wanted to look away of course, but I forced myself to stay focused and remember that I was only looking at Mike's corpse. Just a vessel, nothing more. The real Mike was over at the scrapyard, waiting on me to solve this mystery. Waiting on me to get him to the other side.

'Beginning dissection,' said Anand, and brought the gleaming blade to Mike's shoulder joint in preparation of the first cut of the Y. 'Making the first incision now...'

The tip of the knife was pressing into the boy's dead flesh—

—When his hand struck out and seized Anand by the wrist.

The body's eyelids snapped open to reveal two gleaming white orbs. His mouth cracked apart and launched a scream like a baby born without skin. It was the kind of sound that made you want to stab out your eardrums.

Anand cried out in terror, jerking back her arm to break free of the corpse's grip, her face knotted with panic. She scurried into the corner of the theatre and slumped to the ground, dread taking hold and leaving her catatonic.

Meanwhile, the corpse raised its arm and turned to point at me accusingly. 'You,' it said in a voice like two rough stones being ground together.

It was far too deep a voice to belong to a child. It seemed I was finally meeting the wizard behind the curtain. The Hooded Man had made himself known.

'Who are you?' I demanded.

'That is no concern of yours,' he replied. The voice issued through the corpse's mouth, which hung open and slack, jaw unmoving.

'Oh, it's well within my bailiwick,' I explained. 'I'm a P.I.'

'You're no *Private Investigator*,' the voice mocked. 'You

work for the man.' He turned the body's white eyes to the heavens. 'For the ultimate "The Man".'

'You're wrong, pal. My bosses are the ones you're leaving trapped in limbo while you turn their bodies into murder puppets.'

'Lies!' he boomed. 'You do what you do in the hope that it will save you from His wrath. You are nothing more than a servant. A toady. A miserable boot-licker.'

Okay, I thought, I got the message with "servant". No need to put a hat on a hat. 'And what about you?' I shot back. 'What's the man with the pitchfork and the pointy tail paying you to express deliver him those rotten souls?'

The mystery man twisted Mike's face into some approximation of a smile. 'I do not come from Hell,' he said. 'I come from another place. A place I was sent in exile. A place I have languished for decades, waiting for my time to come again.'

His constant deflections were really getting on my tits. 'Enough with the chit-chat and tell me who you are.'

'You already know who I am,' he replied. 'My name has diminished in power, but now, in this time of strife and uncertainty, with the Doomsday Clock at two minutes to midnight, it is on the tip of everyone's tongues.'

'Not mine, mate. I don't know you from Adam.'

The corpse made a gurgling sound that I guessed for a chuckle. 'It humours me that you should mention the First Man. He lived for many hundreds of years, so he did, but the day still came that he had to pay the ferryman.'

The bloke was making no sense. Was he telling the truth when he said he'd been held prisoner for decades? Was forced confinement the reason he was acting mad as a bag of spiders? 'At this point, I don't really care who you are,' I told him, 'I just need you to pack in the murdering and fess up to the damage you've done.'

'And how do you plan to punish me exactly?' he asked. 'Are you going to "run me in", *Detective* Fletcher? Hand me over to the authorities?' He raised Mike's dead, feeble arms, wrists pressed together, daring me to take him away. 'You have no power over me, phantom. This game is far too rich for your blood. Take your chips and cash out now before it is too late.'

'Listen here,' I said, squaring up to him. 'This is my patch, and I'm not going to let some jumped-up Dr. Frankenstein run around butchering people.'

'What do you care?' he asked. 'Were my victims not deserving of their fates?'

Now it was my turn to deflect. 'What about the people you didn't send to Hell? What about the two innocent souls you left trapped here on Earth?'

'That is not my will, that is God's will.' The corpse's head cocked to one side as if paying me special attention. 'The Devil claims his own, and yet the Almighty is content to let his flock linger here on Earth instead of bringing them home to their final reward. Have you ever asked yourself why that is, Detective? Why He allows the spirits of the innocent to remain trapped between this world and the next? The victims. The waifs and strays. The wretched refuse. The people like you.'

'There are no people like me,' I replied.

'You may have a point there,' he said. 'You're certainly the first ghost detective I've ever met.'

'Kill one more person and I'll be the *last* ghost detective you ever meet.'

The corpse grinned like a split watermelon. 'That's good,' cackled the mystery man within. 'That's very good!'

The possessed cadaver convulsed, shoulders shaking with cruel pleasure. Mocking laughter rang hard off the cold, ceramic tiles of the theatre, making surgical instruments rattle and dance in their trays, and then just as quickly as it had begun, the corpse's eyelids snapped shut and the body slumped on to its slab, still once more.

15

I was shaken by my run-in with the Hooded Man, but nowhere near as shaken as Dr Anand was. To save her spending the rest of her life in a rubber room, I spent a little time in her brain before I took off, clearing her browser history, so to speak. Now, whenever she reflects on the events of that evening, all she'll see are mundane, workaday memories of her cutting up a dead child.

And I thought my job was weird.

Since it was obvious that the Hooded Man planned to strike again, I needed to get ahead of his game. If I could figure out who he planned to off next, maybe I could catch him in the act, and though I still didn't understand his motive, I was starting to get a pretty clear picture of his MO. So long as he followed his existing pattern, the next victim would be another one due for the bottomless pit, and his killer the one he'd wronged. That narrowed things down by quite a margin.

It was late still, but there was no time to waste. I picked up the phone and got Stronge on the blower.

'Do you have any idea what time it is?' she slurred from the other end of the line.

'Time to rock and roll,' I told her. 'Listen, I need you back at the station and up to your nuts in that HOLMES suite.'

The HOLMES system is an investigation database that allows officers up and down the country speedy access to criminal activity logs.

After Stronge was finished shouting at me, she eventually dragged her arse to the office and called me from the control room. 'What am I looking for, Fletcher?'

'The Hooded Man is going to need a new puppet. I need you to let me know about any murders that have happened in the last twenty-four hours.'

The phone went silent except for the *clackety-clack* of keyboard strokes, then eventually Stronge picked up the conversation. 'Nothing,' she reported.

'Really?'

'What do you want? This is London, not the Gaza bloody Strip.'

I sighed. 'Roll back another twenty-four hours.'

Again, more tapping. 'Still nothing.'

'Damn it.'

'Do I need to remind you that no murders in forty-eight hours is actually good news?'

Maybe it was, but it was going to make the search for the Hooded Man a fuck sight harder. 'Forget about murders then. Check for suicides, suspicious deaths. Is there anything that jumps out at you? Anything at all?'

The wait was a lot longer this time, but I wasn't going anywhere.

'There's this,' she said. 'It only happened a couple of

hours ago so the details are still coming in, but five pensioners just wound up dead.'

'All at once? How?'

'Says here suspected carbon monoxide poisoning. Happened in a care home they were all living in. There's a note attached saying the landlord's under investigation.'

'Why?'

'Relatives of the deceased reckon they complained at him for weeks that something was up with the boiler, but he fobbed them all off.'

That definitely got my spectre-sense tingling. Fresh meat with a grudge to settle? This was right up the Hooded Man's alley.

'So what now?' asked Stronge. 'Go stake out the dead OAPs?'

'I'll do that,' I replied. 'You go find the landlord and keep him out of harm's way.'

'Sod that for a game of soldiers. So long as our man's going corpse shopping, that's where I'm at.'

'No,' I said. 'We can't have another man getting killed. Someone has to look after him in case our hoodie's already making a move.'

'Then I'll put a couple of uniforms on him—'

'No!' I told her, putting my foot down. 'I need someone I can trust over there. It has to be you, Kat.'

I couldn't tell her the truth. Stronge was a tough old bird, and if I let on that I was sending her on a wild goose chase to keep her out of trouble, there was no way she was going to give in. The Hooded Man was going to be where those bodies were—I could feel it—and I wasn't about to put her in the middle of a boss fight. No, I couldn't lose her that way. Kat was too important for that. She was my best link to the land of the living. She was a damned fine copper. She was my friend.

'Why are you doing this, Jake? I thought we were partners.'

It pained me to say what I said next, but I had to get her off my case, and since pissing off women was a speciality of mine, that's the arrow I drew. 'We're not partners, Stronge. DC Maddox is your partner. I'm the dead bloke you pester when you run into a tight spot.'

'That's not true—'

'It is and you know it. Now go take care of the living and leave the supernatural stuff to me.'

'Forget it. I'm not letting you push me to the sidelines while—'

'Just tell me where the bodies are so I can take this guy down.'

'No, you listen to—'

'We're running out of time here.'

'This isn't the way—'

'Just do your fucking job, Kat!'

She went quiet. Eye of the tornado quiet. 'Camden Crematorium,' she hissed. 'Next to St. Pancras Old Church.'

'Thank you,' I said, but she'd already ended the call.

I let out a long sigh.

Kat's anger I could handle. Her death I could not.

Between running around after the bad guy and trying to stay ahead of my avenging angel, I couldn't tell whether I was coming or going. One minute I was doing the chasing, the next I was being chased.

I felt like a ghost running around in a maze after Pac Man, and as a fellow phantom, that's a pretty spot-on analogy.

Since the morgue was at capacity, the bodies of the OAPs were being kept overnight at the nearest available cold storage unit, which belonged to the parish crematorium.

I called Stella Familiar on my way there. I wasn't going to risk dropping Stronge into the danger zone, but Stella lived for this stuff. Literally; she was created by a coven of witches for the specific purpose of fighting fiends and battering bogeymen.

Lucky for me, she picked up the phone this time, and since she still owed me a favour, agreed to put aside a job of her own and do a little moonlighting on my behalf.

'Thanks for coming, Stella.'

'You're welcome,' she replied, 'especially since it sounds like you're completely out of your depth.'

Now I think about it, Stella stayed "off-camera" during our opening chapter, so I didn't feel the need to describe her for you. Let me remedy that now by putting a picture in your head. I'll start by saying this: when that coven of witches built Stella, they built her *right*. She has the kind of beauty you see on a billboard for a fancy hair conditioner; flawless skin, legs for days, and an arse that could broker an international peace treaty. Even more impressively, she seems somehow oblivious to her own physical qualities, as though she's too modest—or perhaps too focused on smiting demons—to take the time to look in a mirror. Instead, she carries herself in an understated way, dressing in a tomboyish leather jacket and wearing her hair straight and unfussy. That arse, though. Hoo boy.

'How's your detective friend, David?' I asked her, thinking back to our adventure in the nightmare realm. 'Actually, is he just a friend, or—?'

'Just a friend,' she replied, definitively.

'Easy, tiger, no need to get testy.'

She shrugged it off. 'What about you? How's Detective Stronge?'

I thought back to our recent phone conversation and decided to move the subject on a notch. 'Hey, check us out, we both have detective friends. You know, Stella, we've got a lot in common, you and me. We should really get together one night and chat about it.'

'I'm busy that night.'

'Come on! We're both Uncanny, we both fight for the same side, and we're both knockout gorgeous. Besides, it's not like either of us is getting any younger.'

'Only because neither of us ages.'

'See, there's another thing we have in common.'

'Give it up, Jake.'

'What is it? You don't like this body? Because I can get a better one – just name your type.'

'You know, you make it very difficult not to incinerate you with a fireball.'

We walked on in silence, but it was obvious she was crazy about me.

I mean, probably.

We arrived at the wrought iron fence surrounding the churchyard. I knew this place. I ought to, I was buried there. My earthly remains had been interred on the grounds after I crossed over, which is a polite way of saying, "Got brutally murdered". That story will have to wait for another time, though, much as I'd like to vent about it here. Suffice to say, the matter has left me a mite peeved.

I peered through the fence. While the crematorium beyond was still in business—if vacated for the night—the adjoining church was closed for repairs. The building had been declared unsafe and forced to shut its doors after ground movement created by the crumbling Roman drains beneath it caused the structure to subside. To date, the charitable donations required to stabilise its foundations and fix the damage remain far below the necessary target. Make of that what you will.

We approached the iron gate that led into the churchyard. A thick chain had been looped through it and secured with a heavy-duty padlock, barring our entrance. I was about to jimmy it open with a bit of kleptomancy when Stella reached past me and took the lock in her fist. A moment later it was dribbling between her fingers like silver water.

'Open Sesame,' she quipped.

She pushed through the gate and into the church's graveyard with me at her heels. As we headed for the crematorium I looked across to the chapel, which was shadowed by a gathering of gnarled trees that creaked ominously in the breeze. Somewhere out there, among the chapel's surrounding tombstones, was my own grave.

Stella caught my look. 'You okay, Jake? You look like you've seen a ghost.'

'Funny,' I said. 'You know, you might just be the funniest witch's familiar I've ever met.'

I was putting on a brave face, though. Truth was, I was bricking it. If I'd done my calculations correctly, we were about to walk into the final showdown, and while I can hold my own in a scrap, I still had no idea what we were about to face. Who was the Hooded Man? *What* was he? A magician? A demon? Some other archfiend of the underworld?

Stella bought us access to the crematorium with the same finesse she'd shown the padlocked gate, putting a fist through its sturdy wooden door and unlatching it from the other side.

'I could have done that without leaving a bloody great hole,' I said. 'You know, what with being an apparition that can pass through solid objects.'

She shrugged and I followed her down a breezeblock corridor covered in a spaghetti junction of old gas pipes. At the end of it was another door, and beyond that, a faint murmuring sound. Without taking a breath, Stella pushed open the door to the facility's cold storage unit.

The far wall of the room looked like a giant filing cabinet, only instead of archiving documents, it housed a stockpile of human remains. More notably, though, was a man. A man with his back to us and one hand pressed against the wall of drawers, palm to the metal.

A man in a hood.

'Stop,' I managed to say.

The Hooded Man ceased his murmuring and turned to reveal a piano key smile. He was young, some kind of African by the looks of it, and dressed like the sort of bus stop loitering youth the Daily Mail likes to get its knickers in a twist about.

'There you are,' he said. 'And look, you brought a friend!'

I recognised the voice as the one I'd heard at the morgue with Dr Anand.

I could see now why the vampires were so quick to give him Fergal's body. He wasn't much to look at, but he absolutely crackled with menace. Not that that stopped Stella laying down the law.

'Get away from there,' she demanded, her fists throbbing with arcane power. 'Right now.'

'As you wish,' he said, and removed his palm from the wall of drawers.'

Now it was my turn to speak. 'If you want to carry on living, pal, I'd suggest putting your hands over your head.'

'Living?' he said, still grinning. 'What is life but animated death?'

And with that he was gone, slipping out of the room's fire exit like a greasy smudge.

'What the f—?' I started saying, then decided my time would be better spent giving chase.

I made for the door the Hooded Man had departed through as fast as my legs would carry me, but just as I was about to reach it, a morgue drawer burst open right in front of my face. With no opportunity to change my trajectory, I pummelled headlong into the thing like I was running into a low beam. The floor and the ceiling exchanged places, then suddenly I was flat on my back and contemplating the drawer's aluminium underside.

'Bastard,' I wheezed, but the worst was yet to come.

As well as using his magic to make the drawer solid to ghosts, the Hooded Man had also tampered with its contents. With the contents of the entire refrigerator in fact.

I heard a pitiful moan and saw a pallid hand reach out from the drawer above. After that came a withered face, deathly skin pulled tight against the skull beneath. Judging by the advanced age of the body, it belonged to one of the pensioners that had been gassed a few hours prior. As suspected, the Hooded Man had set the wheels in motion for another vigilante attack.

The eyes of the dead pensioner flicked open to reveal two luminous orbs that burned like white-hot marbles. He began to clamber from his drawer, and I just about managed to roll aside before his bare, toe-tagged foot stepped on my face.

More drawers slid open—five in total—spewing out fresh, moaning corpses with malice on their minds.

The Hooded Man had done a swifty, that much I was sure of. The question now was what were we going to do about the killers he'd left in his wake?

The oldies turned to me in unison, their five sets of eyes boring into me like hot drill bits. Apparently, I'd been promoted to the top of the Hooded Man's hit list. Number one with a bullet.

'Any chance you want to do something about that?' I asked Stella, pointing at the flock of naked murder-fogeys coming my way.

'What do you want me to do?' she asked.

'Well, you could start by magicking them away before they have my throat out.'

Undead could hurt undead. Rules of the game.

'They're people,' said Stella. 'I protect people, not destroy them.'

'Those aren't people!' I cried. 'They're dead bodies being used as puppets. There's more life in a eunuch's ballbag!'

The mouldy oldies continued to advance on me, ponderously slowly. They came like a tide of encroaching lava, backing me into a corner, which I was surprised to find completely solid. The Hooded Man had turned the whole of the room super-corporeal.

'Come on, Stella. Get it together.'

'I see their souls,' she said. 'I see their emotions burning bright...'

'Those aren't emotions, love, he's doing a number on you.'

It was plain as day to me, but something the Hooded Man had done was throwing Stella for a loop. He was preying on her responsibilities as London's guardian, taking advantage of her code, tricking her into believing these were people we were facing and not just empty vessels.

The monster mash was upon me now. Naked pensioners pressed me into the corner of the room, clawing at my body, digging into my flesh. I tried to get away from them by translocating but there was too much magical static in the room, so instead of reappearing on the opposite side of the unit, I went briefly out of alignment then snapped back into focus.

Including the angel, that was the second person that had pulled that stunt on me now, and I enjoyed it just as much this time as I had the first.

I fought against my attackers but they were too strong, juiced by the Hooded Man's murder magic. They fought like barbarians, relentless and savage, battering me with fists like anvils. I put up my arms to defend myself, but the rain of blows smashed me to the ground.

'For Chrissakes, Stella... those aren't people...'

Hearing me, she raised a fist, which fizzed and sparked like a welder's torch. She'd drawn a lethal payload of magic from the room but lacked the certainty to unleash it. Instead, she held it inside of her, clutching on to it, too unsure to pull the trigger.

Meanwhile, the juiced geriatrics piled on top of me, one on the next like a playground bundle. The mountain of bodies weighed hard and heavy, mashing me into the floor, pressing down like a giant boot on my ribcage.

Through the cracks in the mountain, I saw Stella, unblinking, horrified, chewing on her bottom lip as she wrestled with the dilemma before her. She'd been built to vanquish evil, not massacre the elderly. No matter how obvious it seemed to me, she just couldn't see the situation for what it was. The Hooded Man's illusion was too stark for her to deny. Something had short-circuited inside of her, I could see it on her face. Stella had gone haywire.

I reached an arm through a gap in the pile and tried to latch on to her ankle, but she stood just out of reach. If I could only make contact with her there was a chance I could take possession of her body and do the spell-slinging myself. Just a couple more inches. I stretched so hard I thought my arm might pop out of my shoulder, but there was no getting to her. I'd have to find another way out of this mess.

Beneath the crush an old woman's face pressed into mine, her features twisted like a gargoyle's. She snarled and spumed at the lips, and the added lubrication caused her dentures to slip from her wrinkled mouth and drop into my eye socket, hard and slimy.

Sometimes this job is not so great.

The rabid old dear closed her hands around my throat and I struggled to get out a few last words before she pressed her thumbs into my windpipe and crushed the unlife out of me.

'Help me....' I croaked. 'Please...'

Stella continued to dither, fist raised but impotent.

I looked her right in the eye and let out one final plea. 'Stella... these people... voted UKIP.'

Finally, she snapped out of her trance, punching forward with her fist and letting fly a mighty scream. The room's frigid air transformed her breath into smoke, making her look like she was belching fire, and at the fulcrum of her punch, a molten arc of blue fire burst from her knuckles.

For a split second, the room turned the colour of an inner-city public toilet lit by UV lamps to prevent druggies from finding a vein. A fraction of a second after that, the whip of fire had torn through the bodies piled on top of me and reduced them to a pile of smoking ashes.

I'm telling you, it was some real Industrial Light & Magic shit.

Stella looked around the place, her skin suddenly pale.

'Don't worry,' I said, putting an arm around her shoulder. 'They were just puppets. The people who owned those bodies are ghosts now, back at the old folks' home, playing cribbage and complaining about immigrants.'

'You'd better be right.'

'Trust me, Stella, I know dead things.'

'What about the relatives?' she asked. 'How will they pay their respects now?'

'I wouldn't worry too much about that. I mean, it's not as though these bodies weren't headed for the oven anyway.'

Stella ran a hand over her face and let forth a long sigh.

'Cheer up, love, it might never happen. Okay, yeah, we didn't catch the bad guy, but we've got him on the run now.'

The fire escape door the Hooded Man had fled through flapped in the breeze.

'What is that?' asked Stella, pointing through the exit.

There was a light coming from outside. I went to have a gander and saw a glow emanating through the window of the chapel across the way. It had a touch of the divine about it, and was accompanied by the faint sound of gospel music.

'Is that him?' asked Stella. 'The man in the hood?'

I felt my shoulders slump. 'No, this is someone else.'

'What are we going to do?'

'*We're* doing nothing. Me; I'm going to church.'

'You can set foot on hallowed ground?'

'I'm a ghost, Stella, not the kid from The bloody Omen.'

I trudged towards the exit.

'Do you still want me?'

'Is that your way of asking me out, Stella?'

By way of an answer, she raised a crackling magical fist.

'Point taken,' I said. 'Now why don't you go back to your coven and let me take it from here? This one's between me and him.'

'Who?'

'A solid gold arsehole, that's who.'

16

Ribbons of pastel light streamed through the stained glass window of the church, settling in coloured pools on the cemetery.

There was no sense in running. Not anymore. The man inside that building was just going to keep coming at me, and for the sake of Mike and Fergal, I couldn't let him stand in my way. I had to get the guy off my back, if only for a little while.

I strutted towards the old stone chapel, cracking my knuckles as I went. I could have phased right through the front door but I wanted to make an entrance, so instead, I magicked it open and forced my way inside. The heavy oak door swung in and its croaking hinges echoed around the empty edifice.

Almost empty.

Celestial light emanated from the chapel's confessional, leaking out from behind the booth's maroon velvet curtain and casting an eerie glow upon the building's dusty interior. I could see the place had fallen into ruin. Thick cobwebs hung on every surface, across chandeliers, across musty prayer books, across a ghoulish statue of Jesus nailed to a cross that stood upon the church altar like a pointed warning.

As I approached the confessional I saw a pair of legs sticking out from beneath the velvet curtain, suited in dazzling white. I entered the other side of the booth and took a seat opposite the wooden grille.

'Forgive me, Father, for I have sinned,' I told the silhouette across from me. 'Is that what you want to hear?'

'I'm afraid it's too late for a confession,' said the angel on the other side.

'How did you find me?'

'It wasn't hard. You've left quite a trail in your wake, Mister Fletcher.'

I suppose I had; getting into fisticuffs with vampires, chasing around after hanged kids and duffing up a bunch of undead OAPs. But then subtlety had never been my strong suit. 'What do we do now then?' I asked the man in white.

'Now we go Upstairs,' he replied.

'You know, I could really do without this right now. Do you any idea what I'm up against here? What this city is up against? How about instead of getting in my way you help me?'

'It is not my remit to help you, Fletcher. It is my job to bring you in.'

'Of course, it is,' I sighed, 'you're a bureaucrat. A traffic warden.'

'You have no idea what I am.'

'Yeah, I do. I know your type, all mouth and no trousers. You act all that in your poncy clobber, but you haven't got the bollocks for a proper dust-up.'

'If I were you I'd shut my mouth before my list of sins is appended to.'

'Chalk 'em up, you pillock. I don't give a monkey's.'

'Consider it done, Mister Fletcher.'

'Good, and how about you go fuck yourself while you're at it.'

'One more of those and I'll forget about taking you Upstairs for judgment and send you the other way myself.'

'I'd like to see you try, mate.'

'Gladly.'

'Come on then!' I shouted. 'Let's be 'avin' ya!'

He shot out of his side of the booth just as fast as I did mine. In one hand he held a set of glowing manacles. The other was balled into a fist.

'Let's try this again, shall we?' he said, coming at me.

I backed away fast.

'What's the matter, Mister Fletcher? Suddenly not so tough?'

I retreated another step and found myself climbing the altar. I'd soon have my back to the wall.

'How would you like to proceed from here?' asked the angel, giving the cuffs a jiggle as he ascended after me. 'The choice is yours: either come quietly this time or be taken by force. Frankly, I'm hoping you'll choose the latter.'

I had no intention of fighting him. He might not have looked like much of a hard case, but I'm sure the Big Man knew better than to send a rank amateur my way. So, instead of putting up my fists, I presented my wrists.

'I thought so,' he smarmed.

He held out the manacles. 'Kindly face the wall and place your hands behind your back.'

I did as asked, turning to face the life-size crucifix decorated with our Lord and Saviour.

He took two more steps to cover the distance between

us. I heard the cuffs ratchet open. Felt chill metal graze my wrist—

And then I went to work.

Just as the cuffs were about to click shut I whirled about, carrying the bracelet to the crucifix and snapping it on the ankle of Jesus. While the angel stood there, agog, I used his surprise to snatch the other bracelet off him and squeeze it shut on his own wrist. It was nothing really. A bit of stage magic I learned back in my breathing days. A simple parlour trick, but crafty enough to get one over on this toolbag.

The man in white snarled and swiped at me with his free hand, but I pulled away fast and moved out of his reach. He delved into the pocket of his pristine white blazer for a key but came up empty. When he looked up again he found me dangling it on my finger.

'Sorry, boss,' I told him.

He strained at the cuffs, so hard he almost wrenched the crucifix from its moorings, but he remained very much captive. I had him at my mercy, for the moment at least.

'Well?' he roared. 'What now?'

Good question. I suppose I could have taken advantage of the situation and laid into the feller, but something told me that maiming an angel wasn't going to get any red out of my account. Instead, I decided to reason with him.

'Just answer me this, okay? How's it going to play with your boss if you pull me off my case and this looney toon murders more people?'

'You're asking me to let you go, is that it?'

'We've been in this situation before, mate, we both know how it goes. You throw some bullshit roadblock in my way, I hurdle it, take down the bad guy, and buy myself a hall pass.

So come on then, what is it this time? How are you going to make my job more difficult than it already is?'

The angel weighed up his options, wobbling his head like a dog trying to shake off a stubborn veterinary cone. Finally, he gave up. 'Fine,' he said. 'I'm going to let you carry on this doomed cause since it will almost certainly end in your death.'

'Thank you very much. So what's my handicap then? Don't tell me, I have to take the hoodie down with one hand tied behind my back? Eyes closed? Dressed like a pirate?'

He smiled. 'No. You're free to continue as you please... with one exception. You must bring the Hooded Man to justice without Uncanny assistance.'

'You mean Stella.'

'That's right. If you truly want to offset even one of your many, many sins, it falls upon you to deal with this threat alone.'

'Who cares how I pull it off as long as I get this killer off the streets?'

'Don't ask me to explain the system. I don't make the rules.'

'It *really* feels like you do.'

He shrugged and made a face that made me want to smack the Catholic out of him.

'Fine,' I said. 'I'll do this one without Stella—'

'Without *any* Uncanny assistance—'

'*Without any Uncanny assistance* then.'

'Good. And when you're done—in the unlikely instance that you don't end up deader than you already are—return to this chapel and call my name.'

'And what would that be?'

'I introduced myself already when we met,' he huffed.

'Be a lamb and refresh my memory.'

He gave me the hairy eyeball. 'My name is Adonael.'

Great. My parole officer sounded like a wizard from a bloody Hobbit movie. 'All right then, *Adonael*. So long as we're done here, I'm going to toddle off.'

'You have twenty-four hours, Mister Fletcher. Go with God.'

I didn't bother answering back, just made for the exit.

'Aren't you forgetting something?' asked the angel, shaking the chain on his wrist for effect.

I offered him a shit-eating grin. 'I don't think so,' I replied, twirling the handcuff keys on my finger as I strolled off. 'Ta-ra, matey.'

Considering he was an angel, the words that followed me out of that church were none too Christian.

17

On the way to my next stop, I rang Stronge and told her that the landlord she was guarding was fit to be released from custody. Much as I wanted to use the conversation to make good with her, she wasn't especially glad to hear from me, and I didn't have time for deep and meaningfuls. Those would have to wait.

The clock was ticking, a lot of clocks, so many clocks it was getting deafening. There was Adonael's clock, counting the hours to my last chance at redemption. Then there were the clocks that ticked for Fergal and Mike and the gassed OAPs, who'd soon be stranded on Earth for good, cut off from the afterlife. Finally, there was the clock that counted down to the Hooded Man's next attack, and there was no telling when the bell would chime on that one.

I wasn't going to let that happen, though. I was going to catch the Hooded Man, whoever he was and whatever he was up to. I still didn't know much about his game plan, but I'd met him now and learned a thing or two about his methods, which were perverse, to say the least. And when it comes to perverse around these parts, there's only one game in town.

The Den.

An anything-goes, Soho fetish club run by a family of succubi. The Den wasn't a place people went to for a bit of harmless slap and tickle. The club satiated its patrons' wildest and most debauched desires, and in return, its owners fed upon their lust, their pain, their unchecked aggression. All kinds of people came to The Den to whet their appetites, and no one spoke of what happened there outside of its four walls. The club's policy of unbridled hedonism, coupled with its open-plan architecture, meant any dirt that might be dug up there was distributed equally among its guests, ensuring an unspoken arrangement of mutually assured destruction. The rare person stupid enough to break The Den's code of silence had been known to receive a visit from a vengeful succubus that served as an apt warning for anyone else considering entering its doors with blackmail on their mind.

The Hooded Man's actions were the behaviour of a sick individual, which meant there was every chance he'd visited The Den, and if he had, Anya would know about it. Anya was the head of the succubus family that ran the joint, and was known to keep records on all of her clientele. It helped her keep people in line and ensure the club ran without incident, assuming you didn't count the wanton shit that went down there as "incidents".

I saw The Den's flickering neon sign looming at the end of the alley. Now, you might think that advertising your illegal Soho sex and violence club with a great glowing banner was a bad idea, but the club operated on a perceptual bandwidth that could only be sensed by a few. Concealment magic kept it out of view of the hoi-polloi – only those invited to be there were able to perceive the place. That way the succubi could guarantee a guest list that provided only the very tastiest sins to feed from. A gourmet menu of filth and depravity.

As to how I know so much about The Den... well, I'm a detective, it's my business to know what goes on in this town. My visits to the club are strictly professional and always above board. I draw no pleasure at all from what goes on in that pit of perversion, no matter how many times I'm forced to witness them, or how flimsy my pretext for being there. Your Honour.

I arrived at The Den's entrance, which was guarded as always by the club's two doormen, a pair of seven-foot tall twins with bovine features and heads as bald as eggs. I knew from experience that they could see and touch me, which told me they were some kind of Uncanny, though, to date, I'd never figured out what kind.

'Well, well,' said one of them, I couldn't tell you which. 'If it isn't the defective detective.'

'What are you doing here?' asked the other. 'Second time this week, ain't it?'

'I've come to see Anya,' I told them.

'She ain't in.'

Bullshit she wasn't.

'Mind if I take a look anyway?' I asked. I went to push past, but one of them put a hand the size of a dinner plate on my chest.

'Not tonight, Fletcher.'

Why the caginess I wondered. I knew it couldn't be anything to do with the way I was dressed, seeing as I'd died wearing a spiffy suit and permanently looked like I was on my way to an important court hearing.

'What's the matter, boys? Got another Tory party conference in? Don't worry about me, mum's the word.'

Probably the *safe word* for some of those degenerates.

'None of your business, dick,' chimed the bouncers.

'I'm going to assume you're using the slang word for "detective" there and let that one slide.'

Again, I tried pushing past, but the doormen were having none of it. I really didn't have time to waste standing around being stonewalled by Tweedledum and Tweedledumber, so I came up with a distraction.

'Hey, isn't that Elton John?' I asked, pointing off to a side street.

While their eyes were busy following my finger I ducked between them and phased through the door they were guarding, leaving them temporarily stuck on the other side.

'Oi!' I heard in stereo as I arrived in the club's foyer and took off in the direction of Anya's office. If I could just get to her in time I could state my case and get those walking biceps off my back.

I speed-walked as I went so as not to draw too much attention to myself, though I doubt anyone there was interested in my presence, even if they could see me. While the outside of The Den looked relatively innocuous, the inside was a hub of sordid activity. This was not a place for subtlety; within its walls, The Den wore its heart very much on its sleeve.

As I passed briskly through the club I bore witness to all manner of perversions. I saw a group of naked people sat cross-legged around a Japanese style dining table, except instead of eating sushi they were feeding on raw fairies, biting their heads off and drinking down the magic inside. I saw a man playing a baby grand made of glass, its insides filled with tortured puppies that whelped musical notes as the piano's hammers struck their tiny faces. I saw a donkey show, except instead of a donkey it was a unicorn, and instead of copulating with a sad Mexican prostitute, it was using its spiral horn to go vigorously at a man's behind.

'Jesus wept,' I exclaimed as I stopped and caught the pervert's face.

It was old B.J. himself, Boris Johnson, Mayor of London. I guess that explained why the club didn't want any snoopers in that night.

My sudden arrival spooked Boris, but not as much as it did the magical mare, who bucked violently at my approach and caused a terrific tearing of the Mayor's rear end. The noise that issued from his guilty schoolboy face, the eyes wide with horror, mouth rigid and wide, fists clenched, nails digging into the palms of his hands deep enough to draw blood... well, it was almost enough to make me forgive him for the broken pledges and endless, smarmy, political flip-flops. Still, you know what they say, you mess with the unicorn, you get the horn.

It was just as I was contemplating this that I was rugby-tackled by the club's doormen and sent sprawling to the ground. The Den's floor was a surface I'd have preferred not to have touched with my shoe leather, much less my face, but there I was, kissing marble that had seen more sins than Sodom.

I fought my way to my feet and squared up to the two lummoxes.

'Out!' said one.

'Right now!' said the other.

'Not until I see Anya.'

They sighed and rolled up their jacket sleeves in unison. What happened next looked to be a foregone conclusion, but as we've already established, I'm the type that rages against the dying of the light.

I gave them a little Muhammed Ali soft shoe to let them know I was game for a laugh. Tweedledum puffed out his chest and bumped tits with me. That was his first mistake. Unlike the two vampires, who I couldn't possess on account of them being undead, these guys I could take control of.

The moment he came into contact with me I transferred to his body and took root in his brain. It was a curiously unruffled thing, small and smooth like a billiard ball. It definitely wasn't human, but I had neither the time nor the inclination to figure out what manner of creature it belonged to. Not when his brother was coming at me with both fists swinging.

I was surprised to see Tweedledumber attack his own brother with so little hesitation, but I was even more surprised when he grabbed a hold of his wrist and tore my new arm out at the socket like he was pulling apart a roast chicken.

There was no pain, though. Usually, I feel whatever the body I've taken hold of feels, but all I got this time was a dull note informing me that some part of my body had incurred a wound. Not a klaxon horn screaming that I'd suffered a catastrophic injury, but a gentle reminder that I might want to check out the afflicted area, so long as I could find the time. No rush.

I soon realised why when I looked down at the stump to see it growing a new limb. What the...?

And that was only the half it. When I looked back at my assailant I found he'd shifted form. He was no longer a bald man with a bovine face but a big green monster with scaly skin, a distended belly and a long nose that drooped so low it hung past his mouth. Likewise, the glamour concealing my true form had also been dispelled, revealing me as a matching monster.

Trolls.

That answered the question of what flavour of Uncanny the brothers were. Trolls were exceedingly rare, frighteningly strong, and capable of rapid regeneration. They were also dumb as muck and loved to fight, which was one of their traits I was only too happy to mimic.

I seized Tweedledumber by the forearm using my regrown appendage, tore his limb out at the root and smacked him with the soggy end.

THWACK!

Revellers looked up from their various orgies, stopping mid-stroke to gawp at the two trolls beating seven bells out of each other.

Tweedledumber jabbed me in the face and knocked my jaw clean from my head, but I'd grown another one in the time it took him to wind up his next punch.

I tore a lump from his scalp.

He ventilated my chest with his fist.

I bit a nice, wet chunk out of his shoulder.

As soon as he hurt me I hurt him back, spraying the walls in oily black troll blood and littering the floor with spent body parts. We were fighting a fight that could conceivably go on forever. A zero-sum game. A no-score draw on a wet Sunday afternoon.

Fortunately, the ruckus was broken up by an onlooker. Unfortunately, that onlooker was Anya, head of the succubus family and owner of the club we were destroying.

'Stop this,' she demanded, reaching into the troll I was wearing and pulling me out by the scruff of my neck.

'Detective Fletcher,' she purred. 'I might have known.'

Anya's office was up two flights of stairs and overlooked the action below by means of a one-way mirror (and yes, it is a one-way mirror for those of you who use the phrase "two-way", because a "two-way mirror" would be "glass"). We entered the room and Anya pointed to a chair. I took a seat there as ordered while she sauntered around her large, mahogany desk and plonked herself down on the thick velvet cushion of an antique chair. There was stuff going on through that one-way mirror that made *Eyes Wide Shut* look like a Mormon courtship, but my gaze didn't stray from Anya for one solitary second.

She was the kind of woman that women loved to hate. Anya's was an overstated beauty that her peers would often describe as "obvious", yet most men described with an involuntary escape of drool. Tonight she wore a form-fitting black dress that perfectly complemented her exposed ivory shoulders. Her long, dark hair cascaded down the soft curve of her back like an Egyptian queen's. Her lips were painted cherry red and her silver eyes shone in the gloom like twin moons.

She was a beauty all right, but that beauty was strictly on the outside. Scratch a little deeper and you'd see Anya for what she really was: a monster that gorged on human emotions, a vicious, hellborn creature that fed on suffering and wicked thoughts. If you ever saw Anya feed you'd be left in no doubt of her true nature. If you saw her eyes turn black, her fingers elongate into claws, her jaw dislocate and slit down the chin, opening wide enough to swallow a man whole.

So why was she tolerated? Why hadn't Stella come in

here and wiped Anya and her kin off the map? Why was this place allowed to operate at all?

The simple answer was that they had permission to. The regular police were blind to the club, and the forces of Uncanny righteousness—who'd once spent decades battling the succubi—had agreed to condone its presence on the condition that its owners confined their activities to within its four walls. Before The Den arrived in Soho, the succubi had stalked London, breaking into people's homes as they slept, sitting astride them and sucking them dry.

And not in a good way.

A succubus drains its victim of their very essence, leaving behind a desiccated corpse, a hollow, vacant husk, forsaken by God and the Devil besides. That's the kind of power Anya has, so it shouldn't come as a surprise that she sent the clanging numb-nuts that let me slip into her place of business back to their post. Anya didn't need trolls looking out for her wellbeing. She was quite capable of taking care of herself.

'Why did you come here, Detective?' she asked leaning back in her chair and lighting a cigarette.

'I wanted to ask if you knew anything about the strange killings that have gone down in Camden.'

'Of course I know about them. This is my city.'

A lot of people like to lay claim to this town, but Anya's claim is truer than most.

'Who is he then? Who's the new guy?'

'Do you really think I'd tell you that? The privacy of my clientele is sacrosanct.'

I put my hands together. 'Pretty please?'

She smiled. 'Why are you interested in this man anyway?' she asked.

'Because he's a nutter, that's why. A grubby little perv who gets off on killing.'

'We all have our peccadillos,' she said, leaning forward to place a soft, slim hand on my wrist. 'Don't we, Mister Fletcher?'

The room melted away.

I was somewhere else now.

The inside of my own brain.

And I was not alone.

Anya was there, dressed impeccably in an ivory dress and long, white opera gloves.

She traced a clean digit along the dark recesses of my mind and inspected the tip of her index finger.

'Filthy,' she said, as she thrust the dirt into my face. 'Absolutely filthy.'

For once it was my turn to have my brain invaded, and it was not a sensation I enjoyed. My head felt full, pressured. Anya was glamouring me. Toying with my emotions, trying to get a rise from me, making me sweat.

A catwalk had appeared beside her now, the kind strippers get paid to parade along. A velvet curtain arrived with it and parted to reveal two women, who strutted out dressed in g-strings and nothing else. They began to cavort and twirl around a brass pole, thrusting their nether regions in my direction.

One of them was Stronge, the other Stella.

'Interesting,' said Anya, licking her lips. 'An Uncanny and a normal. You have broad tastes, Mister Fletcher. Let's broaden them some more...'

The fantasy versions of Stronge and Stella embraced and went at each other like a couple of piranhas in a feeding frenzy. Then suddenly I wasn't just a spectator, I was part of it, a man sandwich, naked and wedged between the two of them while Anya looked on with lascivious eyes. It was some real 18 Certificate stuff. Pure gonzo.

Pulling myself out of that fantasy might be the hardest thing I've ever had to do. Nevertheless, I gave it everything I had and succeeded in pushing Anya out of my brain. Or maybe she decided she'd had her fun and left the insides of my skull of her own free will. I very much suspect the latter.

We were back in her office now, sat across from each other, her dressed in black again, me with my tackle safely tucked away. It felt hot in there. Was it hot? It sure felt hot.

For a moment Anya's eyes were all black, then the whites returned like milk poured into two buckets of pitch. 'I like ghosts,' she told me, taking a casual drag on her cigarette. 'So much fun.'

'Thanks,' I said, hoping she didn't notice the quaver in my voice.

'You exist in the in-between,' she continued, 'on the cusp of pleasure and pain, straddling life and death, a human stroke and choke. Tell me, phantom man, what is that like? How does it feel to walk with one foot on the primrose path? Are your sensations intensified? Your thrills heightened? I must know.'

'I have my fun,' I told her. 'You should have seen me the other day, I absolutely murdered a tube of Pringles.'

Her lip curled and she slumped back in her chair, disillusioned.

It was as good a time as any to bring the conversation back on track. 'If you won't tell me who the hooded perv is, at least help me catch him.'

'He's no pervert,' Anya snapped. 'He kills for justice, not for pleasure. It's not about kinks or taboos with him, it's about black and white. Good and evil.'

'How do you know all this?'

'Because I've studied his needs, Mister Fletcher, and found his tastes to be strictly vanilla.'

She certainly looked disappointed. 'What's the matter, Anya, murder not dirty enough for you?'

She snorted. 'There's nothing carnal about this man's desires. He doesn't do what he does to get off, he does it because he's working to a plan, and there's nothing less sexy than a plan.'

'Fine,' I said, 'but how is any of this going to help me catch the bloke?'

'I don't recall saying I'd help you,' she said, firing a plume of smoke above her head.

I was wasting my time. I pushed back my chair and stood up. 'Thanks a lot, Anya. As usual, you've been absolutely no help at all.'

I was almost at the door when she called after me. 'Let me give you a piece of advice, Detective Fletcher. This world is made up of submissives and dominators, of those who take, and those who give. It's time you asked yourself this: are you a top or a bottom?'

I pushed open the door, but she wasn't done.

'One last thing before you go, Detective.'

'Yeah?'

'Darken my door again I'll torture what remains of your raggedy little soul until the end of days.'

18

Anya couldn't be seen to be helping the law, but she'd done just that. It was in her own interests after all. The Hooded Man killing perverts on her patch was shrinking her client base, and that was bad for business. No wonder she'd offered me the veiled advice.

She knew what I had to do, even if I didn't. She knew I had to take control of the situation. To climb on top of things. The whole time I'd been on this case I'd been thinking I was being proactive, but the truth was I'd been following the Hooded Man's lead from the start. If I was going to get this guy I'd need to wrest control from him, and since I already knew what his game was, I knew how to intercept it.

I had a plan.

Now all I needed was the means.

I was able to visit Jazz Hands at her usual hangout since the angel Adonael was no longer snapping at my heels.

'Well well,' she said as the shop bell tinkled. 'The prodigal son returns.'

I didn't have time for pleasantries, so I skipped straight to the point. 'D'you have it?' I asked.

I'd phoned ahead with a special order. Something to help me put the Hooded Man out of commission once and for all.

'Perhaps,' she teased. 'But first, what's in it for me?'

'Well, for one thing, you'll save yourself an absolutely shocking Yelp review for that dodgy grenade you lumbered me with.'

It wasn't a real threat. I knew I'd get what I wanted from Jazz Hands for one simple reason: because behind that moth-eaten jumper she wore was a heart the size of a family hatchback.

'Here,' she said, sliding a slim metal box across the counter. 'I won't ask what it's for.'

'Probably best you don't,' I agreed, taking the box and slipping it into my inside pocket.

'Is that everything?' she asked, eager to return to her copy of *Hello!* Magazine.

'Just one more thing,' I said, pointing to a nearby vase of wildflowers.

I visited DCI Stronge at the nick. We had a rule about that. The rule was that I didn't do it. Consequently, it came as no surprise when she angrily ushered me into her office and whipped down the Venetians.

'What are you doing here?' she hissed.

It was after hours, so besides herself, there were only a couple of cleaners doing the rounds, but Stronge wasn't one to take chances.

'I need your help,' I whispered.

Her face didn't soften one bit, which only made her look sexier somehow. I blamed Anya for that. It was hard to look at Kat the same way after those images the succubus had planted in my head... *hard* being the operative word.

'What's changed?' Stronge asked, folding her arms.

'I know how to get him now. The Hooded Man. He's working to a system, one that we can disrupt.'

'*We?*'

'Come on, Kat, help me take this guy down. Help me ruin this guy.'

She stared at me, eyes made of flint. 'Well, if there's one thing you're good at, Fletcher, it's ruining things.'

'You're right. You're right and I was wrong, okay? I shouldn't have shut you out of this. The truth is, I need you just as much as you need me.'

I wasn't lying. I needed her cooperation to pull this off, and though Adonael had forbidden me from getting any backing from Stella, he hadn't said anything about getting assistance from a normal.

I produced a bunch of flowers from my pocket. 'So what do you say, Kat? Can we be partners again?'

'Where did you get those? A graveyard?'

'As a ghost, I find that notion offensive.'

She took the flowers and pitched them into the closest thing she had to a vase: a half-full mug of coffee. 'Go on then, what's this big plan of yours?'

Thank Christ, she was on board. I did what I could to stop a great big smile from spreading across my face, but only half succeeded. I took a chair and suggested she did the same. 'Tell me this: have you ever hated someone so bad you thought about killing them?'

'How about every ex I've ever had?'

'I'm serious. I need to know if you've ever thought about *actually* sticking a knife in someone.'

'No,' she said, matter-of-factly.

'Come on, Kat. Everyone has at some point. I know there's not a day goes by that I don't dream of pipping my killer to the post.' I passed my phantom hand through her desk for effect.

'There is... one guy,' she said, making a face like she was experiencing a bowel movement. 'We met at college. He got me drunk one night and... well.'

I almost asked, *"Well what?"* but the look in her eyes made everything click into place. 'Oh, Kat, I'm sorry, I—'

'He didn't get away with it. He might have, though, if I hadn't stuck my house keys in his face.'

Figured she'd fight back. The woman had a real set of ovaries on her. 'Well, did they do him for it?'

She laughed. It was a beaten, sad little laugh. 'No. They actually came after me for it in the end.'

'What?'

'His daddy was some big deal lawyer, and he knew the best defence his son had was a good offence. So, instead of waiting for me to press changes, the piece of shit had me written up for assault. Told the police we'd gotten into a verbal and that I'd gone at him with a knife. At the end of the day, it was my word against his, and he took me for every penny I had. Well, every penny my *parents* had. That's why they live out in Gravesend and I send them the best part of my pay packet every month.'

Same old story, the rich trampling the poor, skirting their way around forfeits and penance.

'I'm starting to see why you ended up in law enforcement,' I said. 'Any idea what happened to the fucker? Since you graduated, I mean?'

'Followed in daddy's footsteps and went into law.'

Of course, he did.

'Lives in London now. Notting Hill.'

'Sounds like you're keeping tabs on him.'

Stronge met my gaze as if to say, *"So what if I am?"*

I put my hand on hers, much like Anya had done to me in her office, though my intentions were a good deal purer. 'I know this isn't fair, Kat, asking you to go through all that again, but... well, maybe we can do some good with it now.'

'What? How could we possibly do anything good with it?' she asked, loud enough to give pause to one of the cleaners outside.

'The Hooded Man. He goes looking for people who hold grudges. If you're serious about wanting to do this college bloke a mischief, maybe we can use those feelings. If you can bring that hatred to the top of your thoughts, right to the surface, we'll be halfway to luring him.'

'And then what?'

'And then I kill you.'

19

'What?' Stronge wailed, foregoing any notion of discretion this time.

'I only need you to die a little bit,' I told her. 'Just enough to get the bad guy's attention.' I removed the slim metal case from my pocket and opened it to reveal a large, brass syringe. 'I'll do it with this,' I explained.

Stronge's "death" had to look genuine. While I was capable of reaching inside people's bodies with my ghost hand and rendering them unconscious with a squeeze to the heart, I wasn't able to mimic death, at least not without actually causing it. No, for this murder magnet to work, I'd need to make use of Jazz Hands' contribution.

'How is killing me going to solve anything?' asked Stronge. It was a fair question.

'It'll simulate a death state and draw the Hooded Man to your body,' I said. 'We already know he's using corpses to play out vendettas, so let's serve him up a nice, fresh one.'

I settled on the church as the staging area for the final fight; St. Pancras Old Church, the place I'd last run into the angel Adonael. As expected, he was gone now, no longer cuffed to the ankle of the wooden Christ. In his place was a snapped-off Jesus leg, lying on the floor of the altar like he'd stepped down from the cross and on to a land mine. Poor guy. Jesus, I mean. As if he hadn't suffered enough already.

I guided Stronge to the altar and she sat down on its white marble surface, back propped against the baptismal font.

'Where did you get that anyway?' she asked, as I inserted the needle of the brass syringe into its accompanying vial of red liquid.

'It was a gift from my friend, Jazz Hands.'

Stronge pulled away. 'Let me get this right, I'm supposed to trust my life to someone called "Jazz Hands"?'

'Jazz Hands is just her nickname,' I assured her. 'Her real name is Madam Olena.'

'Oh, in that case, go ahead and pump my veins with your magical death juice.'

I laughed and drew back a dose. 'Don't be so dramatic, I have the antidote right here.' I shook a vial of bilious green liquid. 'Soon as the big bad shows up I'll shoot you full of the good stuff and we'll take him out together.' I set down the green vial that Jazz Hands had assured me would act as a remedy to Stronge dying.

She rolled up her sleeve. 'What do we do when he gets here? The Hooded Man I mean.'

'Let me worry about that.'

'Thanks, but if it's all the same with you, I thought I'd bring along a little insurance policy.'

She reached into her jacket and pulled out a gun.

'Whoah, you came tooled up?' I asked, and then, 'Wait a second, is that my shooter?'

It was. My pearl-handled revolver, the one Jazz Hands had given me to use against the soul feaster. I hadn't seen it since I was framed for murder and the boys in blue took it off me. You know, sometimes when I see a sentence like that, I realise I lead a pretty exciting life.

'What are you doing with my pistol?' I asked.

'Smuggled it out of the station's evidence locker,' Stronge explained.

'Thanks,' I said, going to take it back, but she snatched it away.

'This is for me,' she said.

'But you're going to be dead on the floor.'

'And I'll still be a better shot than you.'

Fair enough then. Something told me my puny six-shooter wasn't going to do much damage to the Hooded Man anyway.

With that settled, it was time to get to work. 'You remember the plan?' I asked.

'Yes. I picture that shit-bag from college as hard as I can—'

'And all the unpleasant things you want to do to him—'

'And then you jab me with that needle of red stuff.'

'Right.' I squeezed out a drop and gave the syringe a flick like I'd seen done on the telly. 'Are we ready?'

Her face went hard as she concentrated on the man who'd wronged her, then finally she nodded. 'Do it.'

I stuck her with the needle as gently as I could. After a couple more stabs and what I would describe as an awful lot of profanity for a church, I eventually found Stronge's vein. 'It's going to be okay,' I told her.

Only once I got a final nod from her—it was Stronge's neck on the block after all—did I press down on the plunger and shoot her full of crimson death juice.

She gasped as the poison entered her arm. Almost immediately the blood drained from her face. She made to draw a breath but it caught in her throat. Her eyes bulged wide as she began to cough and choke. It was hell to watch her suffer like that, her hands snatching at me, her fingers clawing the air like the branches of a storm-tossed tree. I made my palm solid and placed it on her rib cage to find her heart had stopped beating.

'It's okay,' I said, as much for my state of mind as hers. 'It's okay.'

Finally, she stopped thrashing and ceased trying to draw breath. Her eyes clouded over and turned skywards as her body went limp against the baptismal font.

Stronge was dead.

I immediately started to scan my surroundings, my eyes darting desperately around the nave for a first glimpse of the Hooded Man. I looked down the aisle. I looked behind the pews. I looked to the vestry and pulpit. I even cast a glance to the rafters in case the bastard planned on abseiling in like some SAS soldier.

The Hooded Man was nowhere to be seen, though. I began to panic. I'd flatlined Stronge, and I couldn't stick her with the antidote until our man had made a show. That left us with just under two minutes of play before she suffered permanent brain damage. I checked my watch. We were already at a minute-thirty.

'Come on!' I said, my voice echoing around the still empty church. 'Show yourself.'

A minute-forty. It was looking bad. I scrabbled for the

green vial of antidote, and in my haste, it slipped from my hand and struck the hard stone of the altar.

Crack.

The sound rang out like a distant gunshot as the vial shattered and spilt its precious contents across the marble floor.

I watched as the green liquid dribbled down the altar steps, *drip, drip, drip.*

It took me ten more seconds to find my voice.

'No,' I croaked, as the antidote ebbed away. I felt as though my heart had dropped through my pelvis—

And then, from out of nowhere, I felt a hand on my shoulder.

'Here,' said the Hooded Man, grinning from ear to ear. 'Let me get that for you...'

He placed his free hand on Stronge's chest, and a moment after that her eyes snapped open, burning white as snow.

20

The shock propelled me backwards, causing me to bounce painfully from the altar's large wooden cross. The Hooded Man was up to his old tricks again, turning our surroundings super-corporeal and making them brick-solid to even the most immaterial of us.

He dropped to his haunches, cradling Stronge in his arms and drawing her into an embrace. 'Ahhh,' he said, nuzzling the soft skin of her neck and taking a deep breath. 'The perfect blend of death and vitriol. It's a sweet smell, is it not?'

'Let her go!' I snapped.

'Certainly,' he replied.

The Hooded Man withdrew his arms, stood, and backed away, but Stronge didn't settle on the altar before him. Instead, she sat up robotically, found her feet and positioned herself beside him.

He looked to me. 'Thank you for your assistance,' he said, 'you're a real lifesaver. Well, you know what I mean...'

I looked to Stronge, but she just stood there, a silent witness. I swear I saw some life in there, though. Some semblance of who she really was. I knew dead things after all, and I could see her soul hadn't departed her body yet. If it had, her ghost would be in the vicinity. No, something in Jazz Hands' potion had sealed Stronge's spirit inside; locked it in good and tight. There was hope for her still, I was sure of it. A way to break the Hooded Man's spell and return Stronge to the land of the living. So long as I put an end to him, I could get her back. I had to believe that. Had to.

'Well,' I said. 'Where do we go from here?'

'That depends on which of us you're referring to,' replied the Hooded Man. 'The two of us will be engaging in a very short and very decisive altercation. Once that matter is brought to a close, your friend here will be making a trip to Notting Hill with that gun in her pocket.'

'That's not gonna happen,' I replied, with way more confidence than I felt. The Hooded Man's victims dropped dead for good once they'd completed their little pantomime, and there'd be no getting Stronge back after that. She'd end up a phantom like me, lodged between this world and the next, dead/alive.

As I was pondering this, a fist struck me in the jaw and left me splashed on the ground like a beached flounder. The Hooded Man had closed the distance between us in a cocaine heartbeat, and was already coming at me again. While I was struggling to reorient myself he grabbed my arm, jacked it up behind my back, and smashed my head into the baptismal font.

Pow.

I reeled backwards, staggering down the aisle, feeling like my brain had been excavated. 'What are you?' I slurred, punch drunk.

He let out a brittle laugh. 'You really don't recognise me?'

I scanned him up and down, taking in his black cotton

hoodie and tracksuit bottoms. 'All I see is some bloke who drives a Vauxhall Nova and lives on a council estate.'

He offered me a rictus grin and regarded his reflection in the stained glass window. 'I thought it was about time I updated the old duds for the modern era,' he said, 'but if it's the classic look you're after, here you go...'

He snapped his fingers and his skin began to bubble and liquify. As he stood there, the flesh poured from his face, melting him through to the bone like a Nazi with an ark. I looked away in horror, and when I dared look back again I found him transformed completely. Gone was the young black man in the North Face sportswear, changed now into a skeletal figure in a hooded black robe. In his hand, he gripped a tall scythe.

'The... Grim Reaper?' I stammered, my voice a squeak.

Vic Lords had been right. I was dealing with something else here. Something legendary.

The Hooded Man's bone feet clacked on the marble as he strolled towards me. 'I've been known by many names over the centuries,' he told me. 'The Reaper, Death, Charon, The Boatman, The Rider of the Pale Horse. Believe it or not, I used to be feared once. Admired. Valued. Of course, that was before the Man Upstairs phased me out and turned me into a... a bloody Halloween costume.' He swung his scythe and lopped the top off a four-feet tall candlestick. 'When I think of all that I did for Him... swinging my sickle, reaping great clusters from the vine. And the work I did here in London during the Black Plague...?' He kissed the tips of his bony fingers with his lipless mouth.

As he continued to advance on me I did what I could to placate him, hoping to buy myself enough time to come up with a plan. 'I hear you, pal,' I said, 'the bloke's got no class.'

'You've got that right!' agreed the Hooded Man. 'And it

used to be so classy! Picture yourself sat upon a hand-carved wooden barge as I stand before you, punting your soul across the River Styx, transporting you to your final judgment.'

'Sounds great,' I replied. 'You know what I got? The old golden elevator.'

'Christ, I hate that thing!' he spat. 'Golden lifts, golden staircases, golden bloody chariots! What's next, golden jet planes? Golden rocket ships? What is it with Him and gold? Ever since He modernised He's become bling *obsessed*!'

'Progress, eh?' I said, offering him a conciliatory shrug as he continued to back me into a corner.

'I tried to keep up, I really did,' he went on. 'Tried to move with the times. I even offered to trade the scythe in for a chainsaw, but He was having none of it.'

It's a terrible day when even Death's depressed. This Millennium, man.

'I get that you're upset,' I told him, 'but why are you making people kill? I thought your job was to collect souls, not claim them.'

'That was the old way,' he replied. 'When death was comfy and quaint. I decided I needed to try something different. Something more fitting for these times. Now I take the initiative. I don't wait for things to happen anymore, I grab the bull by the horns.'

He sounded like a madman; worse, like a contestant auditioning for *The Apprentice*. 'Can't you just let things be?' I asked. 'Why get involved at all? Why not just move on with your life? Hit the links. Go on a cruise. Do a Sudoku.'

'No!' he roared. 'I'm going to get His attention. I'm going to make Him see I've still got it. I'm going to get my job back.'

I cast a quick glance to Stronge, who stood rooted to the spot still, like a pawn awaiting a game of chess.

'You used a dead kid to murder a man,' I told the Hooded Man. 'What do you think God's going to make of that?'

'Don't be so squeamish, the boy was already dead. Besides, I needed to make a grand gesture. God doesn't notice the details, there are too many souls on this Earth for Him to be a micromanager. He only cares about the big picture now, and that's what I'm giving Him – something worthy of His attention. Something biblical.'

This was beginning to turn into a real Ted Talk. 'You've lost it,' I told him. 'You really have.'

'I just wanted to get in His good graces,' the Hooded Man pleaded. 'Surely you of all people should understand that?'

He had a point there. We were both chasing the same goal to some degree, the only difference was that he was off his rocker. Being stuck in limbo had really done a number on this feller. Was that going to be me one day I wondered? Gone loopy from being trapped in a dimension I didn't belong?

'We're nothing like each other,' I told him, as much for my sake as his. 'I help people. You only help yourself.'

His skull seemed to smile, though I'm not sure how. 'I can see the contents of a man's soul, Mister Fletcher, and yours... yours is not so pure.'

'It's clean enough,' I replied. 'Now are you going to put my friend back to normal or are you and me going to have a falling out?'

It was all bluster, really. I'd rather have been anywhere but in that church giving the large to the Grim Reaper himself, but I had to stand tall. Stronge stood there, pale and lifeless, her very existence on the line. I'd led her into this mess and I was damned if I wasn't going to lead her out of it. I'd made up my mind; tonight *I* was the ferryman, and I was boating the other way.

The Hooded Man rapped the wooden part of his scythe on the floor as if to say, "That settles that then", then he raised the large, curved blade and presented it like a giant metal frown. 'Take one last look at your surroundings, Mister Fletcher, because this is as near to Heaven as you're ever going to get.'

He brought down the scythe and I dodged it with a hair to spare. He swept it in a horizontal arc next, and I only managed to pull clear of that one by sucking in my gut. We went on like that for a little while, me bobbing and weaving while he carved up the place. Pews were scarred, a donations box obliterated, a bowl overturned, spilling communion wafers everywhere (or "Jesus crackers" as I like to call them). Each time he missed me I lunged at him for a jab, but no amount of welterweight boxing was going to upset the personification of death itself.

Soon enough my luck ran out and my futile struggle came to an end. The Hooded Man surprised me by using the wooden part of the scythe (the "snath," Google tells me) to hook my legs out from under me and deliver me to the ground.

Wallop.

I landed hard on my tailbone, but before I could voice my displeasure, I saw the Hooded Man's fatal farm tool come driving down on my neck. Somehow I found the wherewithal to defend myself, reaching for the back of a pew and grabbing the first thing that came to hand: a holy bible.

The Reaper's scythe bit into the book and made it about

as far as Second Corinthians. Because of the angle, he was only able to employ the back part of the blade (the "rib" – thanks again, Google), so thankfully he didn't slice right through.

'Help me!' I shouted, as the Hooded Man pushed down on the blade some more and cleared his way to Ephesians.

'Who are you calling?' he asked. 'Her?' His hollow eye sockets flicked to Stronge, who stood there statue-still, jaw slack.

'You're just going to let this happen?' I screamed. 'You're going to let this fruitcake do me in, is that it?'

The Hooded Man put his full weight on the scythe, pushing the blade all the way through to Hebrews. 'Or is it the other one you're calling? Your Uncanny friend, the witch's familiar?'

The blade split open the book of John. The only thing standing between me and my maker now was John's Epistles, a flimsy bit of correspondence stuffed into the back of the bible to bump up the page count. 'Come on!' I yelled. 'What are you waiting for?'

'No one's coming to help you, ghost.'

It was certainly starting to look that way. I had one last chance to get myself out of this before I wound up deader than a character played by Sean Bean. 'My life for hers!' I croaked, my eyes shooting to Stronge.

The rib of the scythe punched through the last book of the bible and into my throat, pressing down on my windpipe hard. I got one hand under it, but that would only buy me a few extra seconds. I swatted at the Hooded Man's leg with my other hand, but the best I could manage was to ruffle his robes.

'What are you doing?' he mocked, as I clawed desperately at the hem of his raiment. 'Do you really think you can kill Death?'

'No,' I squeaked. 'But he can...'

The Hooded Man turned to see a celestial glow shooting out from the church's confession booth, and then its curtain open in one swift swipe.

I'd chosen this arena for a reason.

21

Adonael the angel stood there in his bleach-white suit, shoulders thrown back, looking genuinely fierce. By his side, he held a sword, polished to a mirror finish. It was the seraphim sword, the one I'd apparently allowed to be burned up by witchfire during my tangle with the soul feaster. The same one he'd been holding over my head like the, well... sword of Damocles, adding its "destruction" to my already lengthy list of sins.

'You little shit,' I cried, seeing the sword intact, and in mint condition no less.

'Next time, don't play with things that don't belong to you,' he replied.

All that, just to teach me a lesson about messing with stuff that wasn't mine. And he waited how long to do it? I mean, I know God works in mysterious ways and all that, but this was taking the piss.

The Hooded Man watched Adonael as he ascended the altar steps and approached Stronge, who stood zombified still, eyes dead as a halibut's.

Adonael turned to me. 'I can return her from the

brink, Mister Fletcher, but know this: my intervention here—an intervention that you have called upon—breaks the conditions of our bargain. Once this is done, I am taking you Upstairs. Do we understand one another?'

'It's a fair cop,' I said.

It was worth it. I'd had my life and then some. My raggedy soul for Stronge's was about an equitable deal as I could imagine.

With an agreement settled, Adonael placed a hand on Stronge's shoulder and immediately her face flushed pink. She gasped and sucked down about five minutes of unbreathed air, then collapsed to the floor like a puppet cut from her strings. She coughed, spluttered, and fouled the air with some choice profanities.

'Kat, are you okay? Speak to me!'

'I can't believe you smashed the antidote, you prick,' she wheezed.

I smiled. She was back.

During all of this, the Hooded Man simply stood by and watched, his expressionless, skull face making it impossible to tell what he made of Adonael's intrusion. Was he angry? Scared? Gently amused?

Adonael looked to the Hooded Man, then to me. 'I'm going to dispatch this wretch now,' he said.

And with that, the angel pounced at the Reaper, his sword singing a high, swift tune as it cleaved the air. The Hooded Man stalled Adonael's attack with his scythe and the curved blade shivered and rang like a tolled bell. The two of them fought, sword to sickle, metal clashing, sparks flying.

It was a hell of a sight to see.

The Reaper and the angel, black against white, yin and

yang, circling each other like a swirl of squid ink in a butter churn.

The two of them continued to lock horns, raining down on one another with their blades, each of them giving as good as they got.

'I'm going to clip your wings, angel!' hollered the Hooded Man, swinging his scythe and drawing a swatch of white cloth from the angel's suit jacket.

Adonael replied by cracking the Hooded Man in the skull with the pommel of his sword and sending him reeling.

It turned out the angel was a bit tasty after all. This was no traffic warden. This was no parole officer. This was a *gladiator*.

The pair of them continued to give each other a proper drubbing. Standing there, watching them go at it, I started to feel like a bit of a third wheel. I considered grabbing Stronge and doing a runner, but I knew that would only end up compounding my problems. I couldn't keep running forever. Soon enough I was going to run out of road.

Adonael dealt the Hooded Man a crushing blow that sent him staggering into the baptismal. The Reaper looked down at the ragged cleft in his robes and arranged his skull into a grimace. He was hurting. The angel took a step forward to deliver the death blow, but didn't reckon on the Grim Reaper being a bit of a wrong 'un.

'Watch out for that—' I shouted, but I was too late.

The Hooded Man reached into a pocket of his robe, scooped out a handful of grave dust, and blew it into the angel's eyes.

It was a move straight out of the *Big Book of Dirty Tricks*, but Adonael, being an apple-polishing boy scout, didn't see it coming. Instead, he coughed and clawed at his eyes as though he'd been pepper-sprayed, his sword ringing from the marble altar as it slipped from his hands. While he was busy with that, the Hooded Man swept his legs from under him, dropped to one knee, and hooked the blade of his scythe under the angel's chin, drawing a bead of blood.

The Reaper let out a slithery laugh. 'If this doesn't get His attention I don't know what will...'

He went to yank back the blade and crop off Adonael's head, but just as his arm tensed a shot rang out, quickly followed by five more.

Stronge.

She stood beside me, smoking gun in her grip, hands steady as a rock.

Not that her efforts amounted to anything. The bullets rattled around the Hooded Man's ribs and shot out of the other side, leaving him completely unharmed. He was as indestructible as Tom Cruise's confidence. All Stronge managed to succeed at was lightly aerating the dread spectre of death.

Wait a minute...

Spectre.

A spectre is a ghost.

And I knew how to hurt ghosts.

The Hooded Man shook off Stronge's distraction and returned to the matter at hand, raising his blade to lop off Adonael's big, dumb head.

I had one more roll of the dice. One more chance to make this right. Moving quickly, I yanked the baptismal font off its pedestal, heaved it over my head and dumped it on the Reaper like an ice bucket challenge.

He screamed. Screamed like a Munch painting. Screamed like a hog being tied for market.

Ghosts hate holy water, or at least the ones with faith do.

It has no effect on me because I'm not devout, but the Reaper... he was right out of Revelations.

The water dissolved the Hooded Man's skull like an Alka-Seltzer dropped into a glass of drink. I saw right through the top of his cranium to a pulsing black brain, which fizzed and popped as the holy water continued its acid burn through the remains of his head.

He wasn't done yet, though.

With a final gasp, the Hooded Man thrust out a hand and slipped it, phantom-like, through my chest. Now it was my turn to gasp as his bony fingers closed around my heart.

'Die!' wheezed the Hooded Man, as the holy water burned through to the hinge of his jaw and left it swinging like a pendulum.

The old hand around the heart trick was one I'd played on countless bastards. It didn't feel good to wear the shoe on the other foot, though. It didn't feel good at all.

I felt my knees buckle and the world begin to turn to black soup.

I looked to Adonael, but he lay there clutching his neck and coughing.

I looked for Stronge but my eyelids were too heavy to find her.

Sleep fell on me like a guillotine.

Then, *CRASH*.

The giant, free-standing crucifix came toppling down, striking the Hooded Man and pinning him beneath its weight. I was delighted to feel his hand withdraw from my chest, and even more delighted to see it lay flat on the altar, fingers splayed and still at last.

I looked up to see the cross-toppler looming over me. 'The power of Christ compels thee,' said DCI Stronge.

22

The way Adonael saw it, it was unclear whether it was really the Grim Reaper we'd banished. Was the Hooded Man who he said he was, or was he just some demonic entity with a screw loose and a penchant for waxing poetic? Me, I'm going with the former. Looks better on my CV.

Either way, the job was done and I was riding high. There was one thing bugging me, though…

'I can't believe you lied to me about the sword,' I said.

Adonael made slits of his eyes. We were sat on the front steps of the church, invisible to the world, watching an ambulance drive away with Stronge in the back. She'd wanted to walk home if you can believe that, but I insisted she get herself properly checked out. It's not every day you die and come back to life. I've been around the block a few times, and even I've only had it happen once.

I looked back to the sword on Adonael's hip. 'I'm just saying it's not very godly is all.'

'What would you know about *godly*?' he grunted.

'Well, let me see,' I said, stroking my chin. 'I saved the souls of the Hooded Man's victims... oh, and I saved your life too.'

Rescuing an angel from the jaws of death. That had to be worth a few Brownie points.

'The way I see it,' he replied, 'it was your detective friend that saved my life when she toppled that cross. And the only reason that happened was because I loosened it from its moorings the first time we came here.'

'—And the only reason *that* happened was because I shackled you to the cross in the first place.'

His nostrils flared at the memory. I had him over a barrel, we both knew it. After all, if he was really going to cart me off to the afterlife, we'd already be well on our way by this point.

'In any case,' he grumbled, 'you still have a lot of work to do before your account is anywhere near the black. A *lot* of work.'

I grinned. 'Who's keeping track of my finances anyway? The Big Man?'

'I keep the tally, Mister Fletcher. The Lord Almighty barely knows you exist. You really think He has time to keep track of the likes of you? You're my job, and one of these days I'm going to close the books on you. Rest assured, this is merely a stay of execution.'

'What good's an execution when I'm already dead?'

'A reprieve then. But if you put one foot wrong...'

'Yeah yeah, helter-skelter to Hades, I get it.' I stood up. 'Oh, one last thing before you go, just a quick one... what does God look like?'

'That is not for you to know,' he replied.

I chuckled. 'You've never even met him, have you?'

'Of course, I have!' he barked.

'You're lying, Adonael. A lying angel. No wonder you got the shitty stick and wound up with me on your books.'

I visited DCI Stronge first thing next morning. It was the second time I'd seen her laid up in a hospital bed, and I very much hoped the last.

A doctor had diagnosed her symptoms and checked her in with that most perennial of Hollywood afflictions: exhaustion. Little did she know her patient had been pumped full of magical poison and brought back from the brink of death by an avenging angel. To be fair, though, even House M.D. wouldn't have figured that one out.

Stronge tried to check herself out of the place, but her doctor insisted on keeping her in for observation. Just as well, really, or I'd have wasted a trip.

'Are those the same flowers you gave me before?' she said, looking at the bunch in my hand. We had a private room to ourselves, so no one was there to see Stronge talking to her invisible friend.

'What do you expect?' I said, acting hurt. 'It's not like I can just pop into the local florist and pick up a bunch of posies.'

Stronge took the flowers and tried to hide a smile. It meant everything to me to see that. She'd been out of it for too long back at that church; how she hadn't wound up with brain damage was anyone's guess. 'They look different,' she remarked, setting the flowers in a vase. 'Bigger.'

'Probably the coffee you dropped them in back at the station,' I replied.

She smiled properly this time. 'You twat,' she said.

And we laughed like the end of a *Thundercats*.

As a thank you for her help, I elected to pay Stronge's friend from college a visit; the one with the patchy morals and the busy hands. I gave that fucker the haunting of a lifetime. The full suite. I'm talking slamming doors in the middle of the night, threatening messages in the condensation of his bathroom mirror, levitating bed, *the works*. Trust me, that guy's never going to get a boner again, let alone put it where it's not invited. It was the least I could do, really. After all, I owed Stronge my life now. Or at least I would do if I had one.

I closed my office door behind me and hung my jacket from its peg. Home sweet home. I slumped into my office chair and heard air escape from its cushion like a contented sigh, a harsh reminder that even my furniture is more alive than I am. I kicked up my heels and put my feet on the desk. I'd been running around town like a blue-arsed fly for days now, but there it was, finally, another job jobbed.

I was with Adonael when he rounded up the ghosts of my clients, Fergal, Mike, and the pensioners at the old folks' home. They thanked me enthusiastically for my assistance, then I watched them step into a big gold elevator and ride up to the Promised Land. I have to confess, I got a bit maudlin seeing them go. Must be nice, I thought, passing to the other side with a clean slate. Death isn't so bad really, it's getting stuck on the way there that's the real tragedy.

But I didn't stay blue for long. I'd done what I set out to do. Thanks to me, my clients weren't stuck in limbo anymore and were free to receive their final reward. I'd done some questionable things in my time for sure, but I was tipping the scales the other way now, even if I had only succeeded by the skin of my teeth. This case was a close one, no doubt about it, but I'd done it. I'd survived. Once again I'd managed to beat death, only this time it was Death with a capital D.

LEAVE A REVIEW

Reviews are gold to indie authors, so if you've enjoyed this collection, please consider visiting Amazon to rate and review.

BECOME AN INSIDER

Sign up and receive **FREE UNCANNY KINGDOM BOOKS**. Also, be the **FIRST** to hear about **NEW RELEASES** and **SPECIAL OFFERS.** Just visit:

WWW.UNCANNYKINGDOM.COM

ALSO SET IN THE UNCANNY KINGDOM

The Spectral Detective Series
Spectral Detective
Corpse Reviver
Twice Damned
Necessary Evil
Deadly Departed
Dread Spectre

The Dark Lakes Series
Magic Eater
Blood Stones
Past Sins

The Hexed Detective Series
Hexed Detective
Fatal Moon
Night Terrors

Also Set in the Uncanny Kingdom

The Uncanny Ink Series
Bad Soul
Bad Blood
Bad Justice
Bad Intention
Bad Thoughts
Bad Memories

The London Coven Series
Familiar Magic
Nightmare Realm
Deadly Portent
Other London
Darkly Dreaming

The Branded Series
Sanctified
Turned
Bloodline

The Myth Management Series
Myth Management

Copyright © 2017 by David Bussell and Uncanny Kingdom.

All rights reserved.

No part of this book may be reproduced in any form or by any electronic or mechanical means, including information storage and retrieval systems, without written permission from the author, except for the use of brief quotations in a book review.

This is a work of fiction. Names, characters, businesses, places, events, and incidents are either the products of the author's imagination or used in a fictitious manner. Any resemblance to actual events, or to actual persons living, dead, or undead, is purely coincidental.

Manufactured by Amazon.ca
Acheson, AB